Dark Horse

Nettie Youcheck must fight for what is rightfully hers, the large and profitable Double U cattle ranch. If she fails, her future will be a life of servitude under the control of a vicious and vindictive father. By her side are just two allies – Hollis, the old, black house servant, and Rita, who runs the town brothel and knows of Nettie's past.

If justice prevails then all will go well for Nettie, but since when was life like a fairy tale? Certainly not with the involvement of Albert Hopkins from the Missouri Savings and Loans Bank, who has his own malicious agenda. But it will be at their peril to underestimate the determination of Nettie Youcheck or her ability to shoot straight, for she is a dark horse.

Dark Horse

Lee Clinton

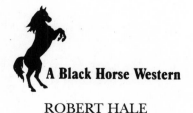

A Black Horse Western

ROBERT HALE

*In adoration of CP & MR,
but who was telling the truth?*

Typeset by
Derek Doyle & Associates, Shaw Heath
Printed and bound in Great Britain by
4Bind Ltd, Stevenage, SG1 2XT

1

AT WAR

Grange, Missouri

'What is you doing, Miss Nettie?'

Hollis had a way of asking a question while scolding at the same time. He did it in that deep gravy voice of his, richly laced with authority to show up your foolishness. It was an acquired skill that I had tried to master but was way too young for such cleverness.

'You know well what I'm doing,' I declared. 'I'm going to shoot him.'

'Shoot him or shoot at him?'

'Ain't it one and the same?' I thought it was.

Hollis didn't. 'No, one is a hit, the other is a miss.'

'Well mine is kind of in between. I'm going to just nick him with a bullet.'

'Then you need to do it quick, 'cos we are real exposed here.'

He was getting anxious, but he had no need, we held the upper hand – surprise.

'We are fine, I was just doing a little pondering first that's all,' I said. 'No one knows we are here, least of all him. Just take a look. Have you ever seen anything more silly? Mister gunfighter? More like Mister fancy pants, skiving around and drawing his gun in and out of his holster when he should be attending to the cattle.'

The lone figure was standing by a small campfire with a burnt black coffee pot steaming. His knees were bent as he pulled his pistol from its holster and pretended to shoot.'Just pondering about what exactly?' Hollis spoke quietly so as not to give our position away.

'About knowing what's right or wrong.'

Hollis gave out a little croak, before saying, 'I thought we was way past that. I mean, is shooting one of your daddy's cowhands, right?'

'We are at war, and I didn't start it.' It was said with a touch of spite. 'And my ponderings were not about the right or wrong of winging a Texan. It was *other* ponderings on what is right or wrong, overall.'

'Oh, I see, other overall ponderings,' said Hollis in a lofty sort of way.

'That sounded snooty,' I remarked while gently laying my cheek upon the stock and sighting on the target.

'Not snooty,' he said in defence.

'Seemed snooty to me.' I closed my left eye and took in a deep breath.

'No, I was just doing some considering myself, that's all.'

I let out half, paused, picked my mark on the outside of the upper right arm, the one he was using to draw his pistol, then focused on the foresight and gently squeezed the trigger. The Henry bucked to the sound of the volley as the cartridge fired and the .44 bullet shot straight and true towards its target one hundred and eighty yards away. The Texan leapt in the air and let out a loud yelp, before dropping his gun as he went to ground to scramble behind his saddle that was lying some five or six yards away.

'Considering what in particular?' I asked and pulled

down on the lever to reload.

Hollis leant over and picked up the spent copper cartridge. ' 'Bout your *other* ponderings.'

'What do you think the substance of those other ponderings of mine were about?' I asked.

'I have no idea,' said Hollis shaking his head slowly.

'You want to know?'

'I would love to, but not now. We need to slowly slide back down into this gulch and get out of here quick.'

'I disagree. Mister gunslinger over there isn't going to come after us. He will be like the others. No courage when on his own. He'll lay there till nightfall, shaking, before he makes a move to run back to the Double U.' I must admit, I was sounding more than a little precocious, but hitting a target precisely where you aimed makes you swagger.

'Unless he bleeds to death,' pronounced Hollis.

'He won't bleed to death, I nicked him that's all.'

Hollis rolled his eyes and went to say something, then thought better, preferring to push back and slide down into the dry creek bed like a snake. I did the same until we could use the cover of the bank to sneak back to where we had left the buckboard.

I never did get to tell Hollis what I had been precisely reflecting upon, but it was no matter as it was nothing he didn't already know. His experiences had not been much different to mine. We had both been born into servitude and browbeaten since young. And we had both just taken it for granted and assumed that was the way it was. For Hollis, it was how black folk were treated. For me, I just thought all men did as they liked, and women did the chores. Men had tempers and women walked softly. Men got drunk and women went and hid with the children. Strange how you just accept what is around you as being the only way it is, when deep down inside that little doubt, late at night when lying awake, tells you it shouldn't be so – that it isn't fair. Hollis knew the same, too.

I guess if you are really lucky you never find out that it could be different and just live in ignorant bliss, believing it can never be any other way. It is certainly far less complicated. Trouble is, I got to see different and thankfully Hollis, being older and wiser, was there to guide and protect me. He was a true gentleman and loyal beyond reason.

My father on the other hand, or at least the man who I thought to be my father, was a brute. He didn't say much, but he didn't need to. A look from him was enough for me to know if I had done wrong, which was most of the time, it seems. And that was when it was best to duck, as that backhander sure could come quick. I took that punishment for years and just didn't know no better. How could I? My mother, Nettie, I have her name, had died within weeks of giving birth to me. I was her first and only child, a girl.

From the way my father treated me I just accepted that I was to blame for her passing, and for not being a boy. The neighbours said he had a right to act the way he did because he was angry at the world. They said he was still grievin' and could therefore be expected to be irritable, a bit. They were fools to think that, but they fooled me, as I believed that it was so, year after year after year, when I should have realized that even grief has a time limit.

I guess it would have stayed that way had it not been for a gambling debt that got my father into trouble. He could have paid it off if he really wanted, but that would have required hard work and my father was a lazy, lazy man. After a night of heavy drinking, he came up with a bright idea. He offered me up as compensation to the man who held the marker over him. His name was Clement

Youcheck, but it's properly pronounced Youch-eck, not You-check like everybody says. I think the mix-up came when his family changed the spelling to keep it simple. Lots of immigrants did that back then, only this time something got lost in translation.

Clement Youcheck was a big man, twenty-four years older than me, and he owned the largest spread in our valley called the Double U. And that was the second reason why my father wanted to marry me off. He fancied that the two properties could be joined up, thinking that he would be part owner of the lot. How foolish, our land was small and rundown. Anyway, Clement warmed to the idea of having a young bride, although he was not so keen on having Karl O'Brian as a father-in-law, and certainly not as a business partner. He knew Karl for what he was, a lazy, drunken, no good, malcontent.

Now, I have never seen myself as one of those wilting lily kinda girls. I was a good worker and could cook, clean, sew, wield an axe, and ride stride saddle like a man, all from the time I was twelve years old. I also had a good natural eye and could shoot straight and put a jackrabbit in the pot from over a hundred yards away. And I could read and write, due to tuition from the Number 6 Public School that was less than a mile from our property. I loved that school. It was my safe haven and I could go as long as all my chores were done, and I had the evening meal ready to serve on the dot of sunset or whenever my father would stagger through the door. Now, six years on, at eighteen, I was strong and confident in my abilities – but I do have to say, I was a greenhorn in so many ways of the world.

The man I had been betrothed to was forty-two years of age and only four or five years younger than my father. I knew of Clem Youcheck by reputation as big, tough and savvy. Everybody in the valley did, and I had seen him from afar, but I hadn't met him and didn't much care to. In fact, my lack of care had me figure that my situation wasn't really going to change that much with marriage, other than I'd be living in and looking after a bigger house. I figured I'd just be changing one old man, who I'd been working for without any appreciation for another. I mean, it couldn't get any worse, could it?

I started to see the light, a little, on that first meeting when I was taken over to be paraded like a cow in a sales yard. My father just said, 'Grab your hat, girl, and come with me.' I'd been filling feed boxes in the barn and still had grain dust in my hair and on my face.

When we got there, I stood outside in the yard and waited while my father went in. Up close, the house was grand but in need of a good whitewash and the old garden beds hadn't been attended to in years. Clement Youcheck came out and looked me up and down and said, 'Do you ever pretty yourself up?'

I said, 'What for? I ain't never been taken anywhere that needed pretty.'

'But you do know how, if you were?'

'Well, I've seen the illustrated magazines and Sears catalogues,' I said. 'I've even seen pretty girls in town wearing rouge, but I don't need no pink cheeks when cleaning out a horse stall or a pig pen.'

As soon as I said the word pig pen, I froze. I thought, I'm in for it now, he'll think I'm calling his place a pig pen and him a pig. I was ready to duck, but nothing happened, at first. He just stood there, silent, and I could see that he had tiny beads of perspiration on his upper lip. He was actually nervous. The corners of his mouth creased, and he began to smile, then he laughed. I couldn't see the joke, but I sure was relieved.

'Come on, give me a big smile.'

I thought that maybe he wanted to see if I could laugh, but he just wanted to see if I had all my own teeth.

'You'll do,' he said.

So, I guessed that the deal was done and dusted. Now all that was needed was to set a date.

What I was to learn later, was that not only was the marker cleared, but that Clement Youcheck paid a kind of dowry to my father of $1,000. A lot of money back then in '89. Seems at first my father thought it was a gift, but what Clement done was to clear all encumbrances attached to this marriage deal. He was a shrewd businessman and he was settling up as he didn't want any further claim made upon him. He even got my father to sign an agreement, and as soon as he had scribbled his mark upon the paper, all legal entitlement over Clement, me or the Double U had been forfeited. In fact, Clement was to take that piece of paper into town and have it registered and held in the bank. I knew nothing of this at the time, but later it was to become very important.

The wedding came about some six weeks later. It could have happened the next day for all I cared, but it was getting close to market time and Clement wanted the stockyard fencing fixed, and he wanted all the cattle going up for sale to be rounded, brought down to the home yard and fattened. He also wanted them clearly branded. His brand was UU.

I didn't know the reasons for the delay at the time, so for a while there, I just thought that he had gone cold on the idea 'cos he didn't even visit. Then out of the blue he sent Hollis, his house man, over in his buggy with a note telling me of the date and that I could use his account at the general store to pretty myself up.

'I'm ready to take you to town right now, Miss Nettie,' said Hollis.

'To pretty myself up?'

'That's right.'

'And I can do it on his store account?'

He went, 'Mmmm-mmm,' and smiled. I liked his smile. Hollis had been blessed with good teeth. They were pearly white.

So that's what I did, and you can still see the results in the picture that was taken with me sitting, and Clement standing just behind and off to the side. That was on our wedding day.

I was allowed to purchase a dress, shoes and undergarments. No limit was set but as usual I remained frugal. Besides, I was never going to wear any of it again so why go to too much expense. Funny though, I still have that dress today, more than sixty years later and I cherish it so. It brings back all those memories of a girl who had grown up in a cage, just like a small bird, but who now had been let out to fend for herself. Of course, I didn't stay like a little bird; I was a child of the Old West and had the makings. And if I am to be remembered as any living creature on this earth, then I would prefer that it be a horse rather than a bird. I love horses. But the type of steed I would like to be is not a workhorse or even a thoroughbred. I would rather be known as a dark horse. One that was running free on the open range and surprised those who tried to tame it, because I exceeded everybody's expectations. Although, I had to do it with some cunning and a good share of conniving. I'll admit, a few fibs had to be told along the way and of that I'm not proud, so now is my time to come clean and make my confession before I pass on. So here it is, as I best remember, this is my story. The story of Nettie Youcheck, a dark horse.

2

A DUCK OUT OF WATER

Oh, What a Surprise

The wedding shindig was larger than I expected – much larger. I just thought we'd front on up to church, say our words before a preacher, sign the doings and be done. But it got a whole lot more complicated than that. Us, being the O'Brians on my father's side, we came from County Clare some fifty years before, although my father was born in Ohio when his family were heading west here to Missouri. Anyway, religion-wise, we were sort of Protestant but more in name than practice. When little, I went to Sunday school, which was with the Methodists. As for Clement, he was supposed to be Lutheran, but that was also mostly in name. The Methodists had the largest congregation in town and the best church, so they got the job, I think by default. Honestly, I didn't much care if the ceremony was held by a witch doctor in a tent. By the time that I was all dressed up in my refinement and taken to town by my father on our buckboard, I was feeling real silly with everybody gawking at me. I had to refrain from poking my tongue out in spite.

The church was chock-full of people and I wondered how Clement knew so many folks because I sure didn't. A little later I realized that they had all come along for the picnic after, as it was all you could eat and drink for free. At that time, liquor of any description had never touched my lips and I wasn't planning on starting, so I sat there and observed a good size of the town having the time of their lives at Clement's expense. By sunset, it was all getting a bit messy and I was bored and ready to go home. Clement had danced with me a couple of times but we both just sort of jigged on the spot, because we didn't really know any of the steps. He then disappeared over to the makeshift bar and I went looking for my father in the hope that he was ready to go. Fat chance that was. When I did find him, he was glued to the bar, so I guessed I'd have to walk myself home, and that's when Hollis arrived out of the dark to say that he would act as my escort and drive me home.

I remember thinking, as I was sitting back in the finery of Clement's buggy, now that is so gentlemanly of him to be my escort. Then when he took the wrong turn down by the creek, I reminded him where I lived by pointing in the correct direction.

There was silence and we kept going before he said. 'But that is the road to your old home. I'm taking you on the road to your new home, now that you is Mrs Youcheck.'

Well, you could have knocked me out of that buggy with a feather. It was then, and only then, that I comprehended for the first time what I had done, or more precisely, what had been done to me. I was now embarking on a new life, in a new home, and married to a man. And as I began to appreciate the consequences of this situation, I started to freeze up. By the time we got to the Double U, I had to be enticed out of the buggy like a mule that didn't want to leave his stall.

'Oh, come on down, Mrs Youcheck, I've got to get this buggy back for Mister Clement.'

'Don't call me that,' I said.

'Call you what?'

'Mrs Youcheck.'

'But that's your name, now. What do you want me to call you?'

'Don't know.'

Hollis lifted his hat and scratched his salty curls. 'What about Mistress Nettie? Would you be happy with that?'

'Prefer Miss Nettie, like you've done before.'

Hollis kept scratching. 'But you are a Mrs now not a Miss.'

'Don't care.'

'If I call you Miss Nettie, will you come down?'

I nodded reluctantly. There was no going back now, that I knew.

'Thank the Lord,' mumbled Hollis when my feet finally touched the ground.

'I heard that,' I said.

'Sorry Mrs—' he checked himself. 'Sorry Miss Nettie. Now please take my arm so you don't fall going up the steps, and then I will show you around your new home. It has been scrubbed clean and dressed up especially for your homecoming.'

'No, I can't,' I said, coming to a halt at the end of the path.

'What now?'

'I need to go home and pack.'

'Pack what?'

'Things. Ladies things.'

'What ladies things?'

'Like, like my hairbrush.' I said. I did have a hairbrush,

15

honest, but I didn't much use it other than to get the knots out.

'You got a hairbrush here. In fact, you've got a whole new dresser set, all laid out for you.'

'I still need to go home and get my nightdress.'

'Got that too. All new and laid out on the bed for you.'

'Who did that?'

'Oh, a lady in town. She selected it all on Mister Clement's orders and she directed me how to lay them out. I wore gloves when doing it.'

'Which lady in town?'

'Miss Rita. She was at your wedding, I saw her congratulate you.'

I did kind of recall a redheaded woman by that name introducing herself. If that was the person being referred to then she was in pretty good condition for her age, if you know what I mean. Heck, I may have been younger and with fresher skin, but I wasn't upholstered with the lumps and bumps she had. The meeting had been one of many, in between a whole lot of unknown faces and slaps on the back, and maybe I had got the name and person mixed up.

I remained glued to the spot, brush set or not. 'What time will my husband be home?' I asked timidly.

'Not sure, but he expected that you would want to leave early. That's why he told me to keep my eye out. I don't think he'll be too long, being his wedding night and all.'

To Clement's credit he had been thoughtful enough to have someone watching out for me, and it was also clear that Hollis was doing his best to help. With a pull on my arm, I edged up the steps and gingerly entered the house. Once the lamps were lit, I felt like I was in some sort of dream but not one of those good dreams. Everything looked big and imposing and I felt like a frightened child that expected a bogeyman to jump out of the nearest closet and scare me half to death. And that feeling didn't go away once I got my nightdress on and crawled into that big crib to pull the bed clothes up under my chin – to await my fate.

I must have fallen asleep, because when Clement and Hollis arrived home, I didn't even hear them enter the house. The first I heard was when Clement came into the bedroom. He held a small oil lamp and put it on the sideboard and asked if I was awake. I said nothing and pretended to be asleep.

I lay there paralysed while he disrobed, each heavy boot falling to the floor with a clomp as he sat on the edge of the bed. I stole a peek as he pulled off his shirt and saw his bare back. His shoulders were broad and the skin smooth in the lamplight. He was a big man but not one that was carrying any lard. His was the body of a hardworking man.

He then rolled into bed and I felt it shift and creak like a ship at sea. When his heavy arm fell upon my middle like a log, I let out a gasp.

'Wake up, Nettie girl,' he said.

'I'm awake,' I tweeted like a little bird.

'Good, cos here I come.'

What happened next frightened the socks off me. He rolled on top and began to squash me while pulling up his nightshirt. I thrashed around in a desperate effort to push him off, before I was suffocated to death, which just seemed to bring joy to Clement, who laughed and called me his bucking bronco. 'You are a strong girl for your size, no doubt about it,' he exclaimed.

I sure didn't feel strong and when he tried to kiss me, I could smell the liquor on his breath and it was none too pleasant. He was also in need of a good shave as his cheek whiskers were like sandpaper. I continued to struggle fiercely and he continued his rowdy shenanigans, having a fine old time, and bit-by-bit I could feel my strength ebbing away. He then pushed his hand down between my legs and I knew I was in for it. I was no measure for a man of his size and weight. My desperation turned to futility and tears welled in my eyes. The inevitable was about to happen.

But it didn't.

Clement fell asleep with his head on my shoulder and began to snore. I lay there, flattened, struggling to breathe and wondering what I would do. It took me forever to squirm out from under his weight, while praying that I didn't wake him. On finally freeing myself, I carefully crept out of that room. Not that I really needed to, as he was in a deep sleep and sawing wood.

I went out to the parlour and sat upon a big cold leather couch and drew my knees up under my chin and began to think. What was I going to do? I racked my brains as I examined every possibility to my predicament. It was clear that I couldn't go home to my father – he wouldn't have me back anyway. So, if I couldn't stay with this monster of a man, maybe, I thought, I could get together some supplies and tiptoe out to the barn and take two horses and ride away – a very long way away – but to where? I had no place to go, and Clement and my father would come looking for me.

As each hour passed I became more despairing. Being back in my own little cot and doing chores from dawn to dusk for my father now seemed like a fairy tale. I would be happy to be a Cinderella for a lifetime and work in a hot kitchen, without ever once hankering to go to the ball.

At the first gleam of light through the long drapes, and still sniffing back tears, I went looking to find a chamber pot. As I crept down the wide passageway to the entry, I saw a handgun hanging in a holster on a coat peg. It belonged to Clement. I had seen him wearing it, not all the time, and not at our wedding, but I knew it was his. I reached up and wrapped my hand round the grip and slowly pulled the gun from its holster. The size and weight surprised me. My knowledge of firearms at that time was restricted to just one rifle, an old Ballard single shot that belonged to my father. I stood there, looking down at the pistol as a terrible thought came to mind. If I were to put that large round barrel to the side of my head and pull the trigger, it would all be over and I would not need to face the terrible fears of married life. I would be relieved of this awful pickle and placed into a merciful and endless sleep.

That's when Hollis took me by surprise and said quietly in that deep voice of his. 'What you doin' there, Miss Nettie?'

I turned with the gun in my hand and started to lift it up towards my head.

'That's loaded,' shouted Hollis with concern and scorn, and snatched the gun from my hand.

I stood there in my nightdress shaking and my bottom lip all a quiver.

'Oh Lordy,' said Hollis, just as Clement called from his room to query what all the commotion was about. 'Nothing, Mister Clement,' replied Hollis. 'I'm just helping Mistress Nettie.'

'Helping her with what?' came the reply.

'She just got a little lost in this big old house, that's all.'

'Umph,' came the grunted response from Clement. 'Well, if everybody's up and making a din, then I may as well get up too. So much for my honeymoon lie-in, ah? Better fetch me some water for a wash and shave.'

'Yesim, coming right up,' called Hollis, before whispering to me. 'Miss Nettie, don't you ever think of such a thing. We can work this out, trust me.'

I will never forget that moment when he said 'we'. He was asking for my trust and while I was still shaking, I did manage to nod my agreement.

'Now, you wash up in the laundry out the back. I'll creep in and get your clothes and bring them to you so you can get dressed.'

'I don't want to put on that wedding dress.'

'You have clothes in your closet.'

'I have? Where did they—'

'Miss Rita. Now hush and go straighten up.'

The clothes that Hollis fetched for me were all new, fashionable but also practical. The skirt was brown, narrow waisted, long in length and split for riding. The blouse was white, trim in cut and with a low collar. The boots, that were a touch tight, were made from calfskin and as soft as a baby's bottom. And to top it off was a straw sunhat with a flat stiff brim and circled by a brown-and-yellow-striped ribbon. I must admit that when I got to see myself in the big full-length mirror in the bedroom, a little later, I was surprised at just how sassy I looked.

When Clement appeared in the kitchen from his ablutions, he was fully dressed for the working day. He was neat, clean and smart in tan knee-length riding boots and wearing a tweed jacket that made him look like one of those English gentlemen out of an illustrated. He smiled, called me 'natty Nettie' for the way I looked, pecked me on the cheek and asked how I had slept.

Hollis looked at me and nodded.

'Fine,' I chirped on cue.

'I had a grand time. What a carnival,' said Clement.

I had no idea what he was talking about. Was he talking about the wedding or his later antics and my protestations? Or had both been rolled into one and totally misinterpreted?

'I'll have breakfast with Martha and the boys, Hollis, so only cook up for Mrs Youcheck.' He then turned to me and said, 'And what have you got planned for today, my love?'

I glanced over my shoulder to see who he was talking to, as no one had ever allowed me to plan my day, and nor had I ever been called, my love, before in my life.

I stood thunderstruck with a dumb look on my face, searching for the answer.

'I'm taking the Mrs into town for some store buying to fancy up the house with a woman's touch,' said Hollis.

'Sounds expensive,' said Clement in a carefree sort of way. He then leant over and gave me a parting peck on the forehead and left for the front door, only to call out. 'Where's my Colt?'

'Holy cow,' said Hollis under his breath as he looked down to where he had placed the pistol on the bench behind the bread box.

'I said, where's my Colt?' repeated Clement from the hall.

'In here, my love,' I called back from the kitchen in a high-pitched voice.

Hollis's eyes expanded to the size of soup spoons.

'What's it doing in there?' replied Clement.

'I asked Hollis to show it to me.'

Clement called out, 'Why?'

This long-distance conversation between the kitchen and the passageway was becoming somewhat tiring. 'Because I want you to teach me how to shoot a pistol straight,' I called back, before taking a pause that was way too long and adding, 'my love.'

'Well, not today,' came Clement's shout. 'But later in the week, if I get the last of the stock graded for market.

'No hurry,' I replied.

'Well, come on Hollis, fetch me my gun,' came the impatient call.

I picked the Colt up by the barrel, handed it to Hollis

and nodded.

He nodded back, then skittled off out of the kitchen and down the hallway to deliver the pistol to Clement.

When he returned, I said, 'What now?'

'I'm taking you to town,' he said.

'I heard, but what do I know about fancying up a house?'

'About as much as I do, and that's not much.' Hollis looked at me and gave his head a gentle shake. 'You are like a duck out of water at the moment, so best we find you a pond where you can learn to paddle.'

I knew I was a duck out of water all right, but I didn't understand the pond thing and said so. 'What pond?'

'The one I'm going to take you to.'

'And where's that?'

'Never you mind, but when we get there I don't want you passing any judgements.'

'Judgements on what?' I asked.

'The other ducks?' said Hollis.

I just shrugged as I had no idea what he was talking about. *The other ducks?* I remember thinking, why don't people just say what they mean. *Ducks*, for goodness sakes, why would I possibly want to pass judgement on some ducks?

3

RITA

A Confidante

When we arrived at the top end of Main Street that divides
Grange in two, Hollis took a turn down Maple towards the
stockyards and the creek. I didn't know this part of town.
The odd times I ever got into Grange was for the getting of
supplies from the general store on corner of Main and
Baker streets, but I was pleased with this detour because I
didn't want to be the spectacle of more gawking in my new
duds. Once past the yards and just after the Chinese
laundry, and along near the Grizzly Bear saloon, we pulled
around the side of the Star Bathhouse.

Hollis asked me to wait in the buggy while he went
inside.

'What for?' I asked.

'You'll find out soon enough.'

I sat there wondering if the pond he'd been talking
about was actually some sort of big bathtub, while casually
watching a number of women working in the backyard,
beating paillasses on a clothesline. On the first floor of the
side veranda were more women, with some of them still in
their nightdresses, and judging from the yawning and arm

stretching that was going on, it looked like they had only just got up. Nice work if you can get it, I thought.

Hollis returned and, with a little impatience, helped me out of the buggy and across to another building that seemed to be an annex to the bathhouse. As I walked past the sleepyheads on the veranda I was given the once over, which was a little irritating, but I did not poke my tongue out at them, not once.

Inside the building it was dim and the corridors narrow, so it took a moment or two for my eyes to adjust. The place seemed to be a rabbit's warren of small rooms with twists and turns, until I was finally guided into a small upstairs office.

The woman sitting at the desk had her back to me. When she turned, she did look familiar with that red hair, and I was reintroduced to Rita by Hollis.

She stood and took my hand softly and said, 'Nettie,' then added in an odd sort of way, 'Karl O'Brian's girl.'

I nodded.

'I knew your mother and remember you as a baby, but that was long, long ago. I've seen you from afar over the years, but you never stay in town long, do you?'

'Have no need,' I said. 'My father does most of the getting of supplies.'

'Yes, he does,' she said slowly. 'And you are now the Mistress of the Double U.'

I didn't know what to say. I had never heard it said like that, but I guessed I was.

'Has anyone explained to you what comes with that title?'

I just shook my head.

'No, I didn't think so,' said Rita as if in pity.

'Hollis brought me here,' I said.

'I know, he explained a few things to me. Was last night

a little confronting?'

I hunched my shoulders, then nodded.

'Has anyone told you about the relationships between men and women?'

I just looked at her, not understanding the question.

'How women get to have babies?' Rita enquired.

'Oh, sure,' I said with a smile. 'I'm not a town girl. I grew up on a farm. I've seen what the hogs and the rest of the stock do to have litters.'

'So, you know what Clement was about on his wedding night?'

'Oh, sure,' I said then paused and looked down at my new calfskin boots and wriggled my toes to stretch the leather a little, and said, 'No, not really.'

'I thought so.' She turned to Hollis. 'How long have I got?'

'How long do you need?'

'In days or weeks?'

'Miss Rita, we are talking hours here, that's all; and we've got to get some prettying up stuff for the house as well. We are on a tight schedule.'

'The girls will help you out with the house paraphernalia while we get some schooling done.' Rita was looking straight at me.

Schooling? I thought, what schooling?

Hollis said, 'Three. We need to leave around three.'

Rita looked up at the wall clock. 'Four and half hours. I'll do what I can.'

'I knew you would,' said Hollis with relief, then he left.

'Now,' said Rita, 'where do we start?'

I didn't know the answer, but I don't think she was expecting one either. She just puckered her lips while thinking, then said, 'Husbands have needs and can be avaricious.'

25

'What's that?'

Rita shook her head a little and clicked her tongue. 'Nettie, men get greedy for things they want, and they don't like to be kept waiting.'

She wasn't telling me anything I didn't already know, so I said, 'I knew that.'

'Well, every new husband gets desirous for what his wife has to offer.'

'Which is?' I asked.

'You.'

I didn't understand.

'You,' repeated Rita, as she brushed the palms of her hands down her sides to her hips. 'You, your chassis.'

I looked at her dumb struck.

'Oh, for God's sake, Nettie, your husband is lusting after your body.'

I'd read about lusting in the bible, but I never saw myself as biblical. 'Well, all I got to experience last night was thrashing around the blankets and being squashed into the mattress,' I said in reply.

'Well, I can fix that. We just need to get Clement to slow down and get you on top. But Nettie, you have to understand the authority of your *allure* and its effect.'

First it was *avaricious*, then it was *chassis*, and now it was the authority of my *allure*. I was confused. I was a farm girl, so what did the French language have to do with me? But, before we go on, I don't want you thinking that I was some sort of prude or a person without desires. I read stories and saw illustrations and pictures in magazines of people holding hands with love hearts and bluebirds chirping above their heads. I just thought that happened to other folk, not me. I just expected to remain a maid. Getting married had certainly been a shock, but secretly I had wondered what such a situation would be like. The trouble was the surprise of it all. It had been a bit sudden and confronting, and not unlike riding a horse and being thrown for the first time. It kind of knocks the stuffing out of you. Could I get back in the saddle? I guess there was no choice, and there were some advantages to this marriage caper, like the new clothes and being driven around in a buggy. It was just the lusting and the French language that was getting in the way.

'*Allure*?' I said. 'I have *allure*?'

'Of course you do. Clement is captivated. He never thought he would find someone like you at his time of life, but he is—'

I waited and had to ask, 'Is what?'

Rita paused before saying, 'Men, all men that is, can be a little impatient.'

I thought that we had already been over this ground on a man's impatience, but if there was more, I had to know. 'For what precisely?'

Rita cupped my cheeks in her hands. 'The pleasure of a woman's nakedness.'

Well, I remember priding myself that I was quick on the uptake, but that Clement, my husband, wanted the pleasure of my nakedness was a complete revelation to me, so I asked, 'What? Just to look at?'

'And to make love, too,' said Rita. 'To have the gratification of your delights. And it can also be pleasurable for you, too.'

'Well, it wasn't last night. I felt like I was being suffocated to death. I've had a stack of chaff bags fall on me from the top loft in the barn that was more pleasurable than last night.'

'Clement is bigger than you, so we need to put you in a position to deal with that. And we need to teach you the power of feminine charm.'

27

'Feminine charm? And exactly who is *we*?' I asked.

'Me, and I'll introduce you to some of my girls.'

'The girls outside, who look like they have only just rolled out of the sack? How would they know?'

'Believe me they know, and they all work hard for a living and need their rest.' Then Rita said, 'They also had older sisters or a mother, which you didn't, to tell of the things you're now going to be told.'

I could see how that made sense, so I nodded my agreement.

Now, I'm not going to go into all the detail that transpired over the next four and half hours of schooling, but it is suffice to say that I was taught the facts of life plain and simple, and then some, which was more than an eye-opener I can tell you. But more importantly, I was taught how to handle a man, well one man in particular, Clement. Rita was to be my saviour and I guess the mother I never had, as well as a confidante. She spoke about the importance of instilling decorum and manners in the household, and of dressing and behaving well, and the need to present myself with assurance at all times. She told me about the importance of patience and controlling my emotions, and she told me about the art of an intimate conversation with a loved one.

'He called me, my love, this morning,' I told her. 'But I don't know why. But he did seem to be well pleased with himself.'

'That's wonderful. He must have had sweet dreams of what might, could or should have occurred. What did you call him in return?'

'I called him, my love, back. But it sounded strange.'

'No matter, that's a fine start. You'll get used to it, and it will become natural.'

I heard a cough and Rita and the two girls with her who

had helped show me some moves, looked up.

It was Hollis standing at the door to the office. 'It's now after three, Miss Rita,' he said.

I looked at the wall clock and couldn't believe where all that time had gone. Normally my stomach rumbles around midday, but the desire for something to munch on had not occurred.

Rita walked me out to the buggy, which was loaded up like a Christmas sleigh with a pile of fabrics, cushions, and I don't know what.

'What's this?' I asked.

'This is only half of it,' said Hollis. 'The boot is also loaded, and a score of other things have been put on order. Those girls you sent to help went a little crazy, Miss Rita.'

'What am I going to do with it all?' I asked.

Rita gave me a hug and said, 'I'll drop by in a week or two and show you how to dress your new home. In the meantime, cut some fresh flowers, it shows a woman's touch, and just put some of these colourful cushions on the couches.' Then she whispered in my ear, 'Now, repeat one more time, the seven steps you were taught today.'

I drew in a breath and commenced. 'Step one, greet my husband and welcome him home every evening with a smile and a kiss on the cheek. Step two, insist that he washes and wears a jacket to dinner. Step three, engage in conversation that is about him. Step four—' I drew in a second breath. 'When we get into bed, ask Clement to treat me carefully and teach me what to do. Step five, accept that it might hurt and be a little awkward.'

Rita interrupted, 'only at first.'

'Step six, don't just lie there and do nothing, make some soft sounds and try to join in. Step seven, let my husband into my heart.'

Rita kissed me on the cheek. 'You learn quickly, Nettie, just like your mother.'

When we drove away, Rita gave me a wave and I turned to return the gesture, only to see the high veranda of the Star Bathhouse completely full of women, all lined up against the railing and also waving to me and wishing me luck. How nice, I thought.

Hollis just said, 'Quack.'

I looked at him, then back at the waving girls. 'Oh,' I said.

'Yes,' said Hollis, 'and that's their pond.'

'And you are taking me back to my pond?'

Hollis just gave a little cough. Was he embarrassed?

He had no need.

I had just been taught to swim.

4

PEACE AND LOVE

What Should Have Been

I dutifully put the seven steps taught to me by Rita into practice, and it all worked out just as she said it would. However, for those first weeks it was a day-by-day affair until I started to get the hang of all this bed wrestling. It was a bit like breaking in your first bronc – you know – one with spirit that wants to show off and buck a bit. Bound to be a bruise or two in a tender spot before you settle in the saddle.

Rita was true to her word and visited me at the end of my second week with buckboard full of carpets, chairs, flower stands, paint tins, brushes and even some wallpaper.

'Lordy,' said Hollis when he saw it. 'I had no part in this, Miss Nettie, it's all the doing of those girls Miss Rita sent with me to the store. They put enough on order to fill a circus tent.'

'They ordered just fine, Hollis,' said Rita as she gave me a squeeze and said in my ear, 'How are you going, sweetie.'

I told her of my bronc comparison. 'It just takes a bit of getting used to. A little saddle sore in places but I haven't

31

fallen off, yet.'

'Good girl,' said Rita. 'See, I told you that each of the steps would work, but where are you at with number seven? Are you letting Clement into your heart?'

I must have blushed because Rita said, 'I see you have already.'

Falling in love is the strangest darn thing, isn't it? He was old, I mean I thought real old at first, but that sort of faded away, because he could be downright youthful at times, even childish – but in a good way, especially when he giggled. I'd never heard a grown man giggle before, but I took it to be a good sign. And he was always appreciative of the things I did for him, and he liked my cooking. Hollis wasn't a bad cook, but he lacked imagination. You don't have to have beans with every meal. A chicken pie in gravy with sweet onions and green peas, accompanied by corn-bread, presents well on the plate – and it tastes as if it could win first prize at the Greater Grange County Fair. Beans is just beans and it gives most people wind.

Over the next weeks and months, Rita, Hollis and I prettied that home up so that it looked like a grand palace. Clement would remark on the finery and homeliness of it all, and I would take good cheer from his compliments. Each night he would not only wash and put on a jacket for dinner, but often completely dress again from his work clothes to those of a gentleman about to go off to market; and a gentleman is what he became.

As the months passed and the seasons changed, my affection grew for this man who schooled me in the ways of life, love and most importantly, in how to run a large property. He taught me what supplies were required and when, and the costs involved for the management of the store account. I learned about the banking arrangements and the importance of cash flow and access to capital for the purchase of stock, goods and labour. And I was educated in how to feed, fatten and present cattle to market at the best possible time for the greatest return. And true to his word, Clement skilled me in the use of the pistol.

I knew I was a good shot with a rifle, but Clem was even better because he knew how to adjust for a moving target over distance and allow for any shifting wind. He instructed me in how each weapon in our gun cabinet worked and how it could be stripped down and repaired. And he explained with patience and coaching how to instinctively hit a target consistently with a handgun by relaxing, concentrating, breathing and gently squeezing the trigger.

'By God, Nettie Youcheck, you are turning into a regular Annie Oakley,' he once told me.

Later, I got to see Annie Oakley in North Carolina. She was older, but it was before her car accident and she was still good and fast, and still setting records. However, it was mostly trick shooting at close range. Without putting too fine a point on it, I reckon I'd more than hold my own with a rifle over the longer ranges of one hundred and fifty yards or more. In fact, the only man who could match me was Clement, who used to say that my eye was as straight as a die. Somethings in life are just natural to some people and shooting was that to me.

The handgun Clement carried was a model 1878 Colt. It was a big-framed gun that fitted his large hand. It was too big for me to be comfortable and never held the *allure* that a rifle did with its long barrel, glossy stock, even balance and polished brass receiver. I liked the Winchester and got to fire the new 1886 express model, but when Clement presented me with a Henry rifle, it took up a soft spot in my heart. It may not have been as flashy or as powerful as the Winchester, but I loved it. Maybe, it was because that was

33

the rifle I was tutored on with its folding ladder rear sight, but more likely it was because Clement gave me that Henry for my nineteenth birthday.

I got dressed up like Annie Oakley that night in buckskins and all, and we had a gay old time, particularly when we drank some champagne and he chased me around the house calling out, 'Here comes Dead Eyed Dick for his Annie Oakley.' What a hoot. I was more relaxed and getting into the spirit of things by then. It's also a boggle what that fancy French fizz can do to your inhibitions.

By our first anniversary my fondness for Clement had turned into a deep abiding love for a mature man, who had responded with affection to the efforts of his young wife to feather his nest and make him happy. What had happened out of happenstance and serendipity had turned into a fairy tale romance for us both. And that's where this story should have ended, with us living in love and peace, bringing up children, and being good neighbours and contributors to our community in the valley. But that's not what happened.

Life is unpredictable, and it can be unexpectedly cruel. It had taken me from a naive girl under the thumb of a selfish father to the arms of a man who loved me with both desire and care. My future looked more than rosy, it was warm in winter and comfortable all of the time, as well as curious and above all exciting. And that was at the precise moment when it ended, to be lost in an instant.

It was the week before the Christmas of 1890. Decorations were up, and the festive season planned. The remaining hired hands that worked the winter were the permanent team and numbered four. During the summer season that number could be complemented by the same again or even more, depending on the head of cattle being mustered and prepared for market.

All of the permanent men were reliable and respectful

whenever I was near. When one would see me coming, he would say to the others, 'Ducks on the pond,' and they would watch their language and lift their hats. I never knew where that saying came from, but on reflection it may have had something to do with Rita and her girls.

The cowhands of the Double U, be they permanent or itinerant, were housed in a barracks-like building between the big and little barns. Attached to their quarters was a kitchen run by Martha, who was about the same age as Hollis. He was also her supervisor and the two got on like a house on fire. I think Hollis had a thing for Martha. I know she had one for him, but I could never draw him out on the subject.

The leading hand at that time was a man named Dutch Bonner, who was a year or two older than Clement and very much the right-hand man when it came to stock management. He was from the old school – a man who said little but could be relied on to see what needed doing, and do it. He had once been married and word had it that his wife had ran off with his best friend, taking his baby son with them. He went searching but couldn't find them and in despair turned to drink. Clement had seen him handling horses and knew he had something special. However, at that time the Double U needed cowhands, not a horse whisperer, but when Clem overheard that Dutch was living rough and drinking himself to death, he decided to help. He went and sought Dutch out and made an offer that would put a roof over his head and a chance to stay away from the liquor through hard work.

Dutch initially said, no, to which Clement was supposed to have said with a nod, 'OK, your call, but in case I don't see you again I want to let you know that I will be at your funeral, so what words would you like me to say on your behalf.'

Dutch was a little taken aback at the offer but responded between swigs of liquor by saying, 'Tell them I was a top rate horseman and that there never was a mount that I could not break and ride easy in a day.'

Clement said, 'I suppose I could say that and it was probably true once, but not now. I doubt if you could stay on a nag even if it was standing still. So instead, this is what I am going to say. I knew Dutch Bonner when he was a fine horseman and an even finer man, but today I come to bury a drunk that wallowed in his distress and indulged with self-pity.'

Dutch's jaw dropped for a moment and then he jumped up and tried to throw a punch. Clement was bigger than Dutch and could have dropped him in an instant, but he just stepped to one side as Dutch's wild swing unbalanced him and he stumbled and fell to the floor.

Clement looked down at the figure flat on his back and said, 'The job is still yours but only until midday tomorrow. Bring both of your horses and all of your belongings. You'll have a square meal each day and a warm dry cot. But don't bring any liquor. I run a dry work camp.'

Seems Dutch looked up and told Clement that he would rather go to hell than work for him.

Clement said, 'That's precisely where you are going, so don't forget to pack a shovel.'

This sarcastic scolding seemed to tickle Dutch, who for all of his inebriation, could still see the funny side of being ridiculed while being offered salvation. And that should be a lesson for us all, keep your humour even when you are down and out.

The following morning, a little worse for wear, Dutch rode through the tall gates of the Double U and stepped up on to Clement's front porch and reported for duty. Clement said, 'You couldn't have come at a better time for me and a worse time for you. Did you bring your shovel?'

Dutch was a little confused and just said, 'Why?'

Clement said, 'We're fencing today and need a post hole digger.'

I believe Dutch said something along the line of, 'Darn my luck, maybe I should have taken that job in hell,' or words to that effect as his language may have been a little livelier. Anyway, he dug thirty-eight postholes that day and fell into his cot before he even got to dinner. When I was to hear this story sometime later at a barbecue, Clement and Dutch nearly laughed their socks off. Dutch was to tell me later, on the quiet, that Clement had saved his life.

During that first year at the Double U I did not see my father but once. It was in town, down on Main, on the other side of that wide street. I saw him and he certainly saw me, but he didn't come over and I didn't go near. Why? Well, I couldn't see the point for either of us to renew our acquaintances, and I guess nor could he. What would we say, anyway? I was also of a sunny disposition on that particular day, most days in fact, and I did not want it spoilt by some surly or snide remark. We had parted ways to live different lives forever, or so I thought.

As those winter temperatures began to fall with the north-west winds, and the snow squalls started to increase in duration and intensity, the tempo of outside work slowed and most of the chores shifted indoors. This was the time to prepare and repair all the paraphernalia that goes with farming and ranching before the coming spring. When Clement said that he was going up the valley to bring down the last of the cattle to the bottom enclosures, I said, 'Why don't you just send Dutch and the boys?'

'I'll take one of the boys, it's just a two-man job. Dutch is laying out all the saddles for waxing and every harness and rope for checking and repair if needed. Then it's on to greasing every wagon hub and repairing any leaking water barrels. He has enough on his plate.'

I pecked my Clement on the cheek and said, 'Now don't you be late for dinner, my love. We are having beef and pork picado along with pickled oysters first up.'

'Nettie, I'll be way home before then and ready to put on my Christmas bells.'

I remember having a sense of unease, but it was fleeting. Yes, it was a gloomy morning. After all, we had just passed our shortest day of the year and it was getting dark by around four. While the weather could be uncomfortable it was not unpredictable, and they had plenty of time to bring cattle down so there was no rush that might result in peril. I had just lit the oil lamps and was cleaning up with Hollis in the kitchen when Dutch knocked on the back door. He had his hat in his hand and snowflakes upon his large moustache. I cheerfully called for him to come inside and get warm, but he just stood, silently, with his head downcast. I went to him to see what the matter was, and when he lifted his head I could see his red eyes and the tears streaming down his cheeks.

'Oh my God, Dutch, what is it?'

He reached out and clasped my fingers and I could feel his hand shaking. 'It's Clem,' he said, 'he had a fall.'

'Is he all right?'

He shook his head. 'It was a bad fall.'

'Where is he? I have to go to him.' I went to push by but he wouldn't let go of my hand.

'No,' he said, 'it's too late, he's passed and is messed up real bad, the cattle stampeded over him. Best you remember him as he was.'

I was in complete disbelief. How could it be? This was all a terrible mistake. I looked down as I tried to pull my hand away and I saw blood upon the cuff of Dutch's jacket. It was

Clement's blood from when he'd been taken down from across his horse.

I don't remember screaming the word, 'No,' as my legs buckled from under me. But I heard it. It just seemed to come from somebody else. Hollis was standing close behind and it was his strong hands that gripped under my arms and stopped me from collapsing to the floor, as he said, 'Oh, Miss Nettie, Miss Nettie, what are we going to do now?'

I did see my love, my wonderful Clement, I had to, and he was indeed a bloody mess. His face had been stomped upon and his body was cold and lifeless. I clenched his hand and wept uncontrollably. My head, then my body seemed to spin and that spin seemed to pick me up and toss me down a deep dark shaft to fall but never hit the bottom. Had I, it would have been a blessed mercy and one that would have allowed me to join the only man I was to ever love in this life. Instead, I just seemed to fall forever with a sense that I was halfway between this world and the next.

The funeral was held on the twenty-ninth of the month with a procession down Main Street. I only remember parts of that day. Fortunately, Rita was by my side to guide me through what seemed like a nightmare. At the graveside in a cold wind and a dusting of snow, Clement Youcheck was laid to rest. He was just forty-three years of age. And I had thought of him as old.

Rita came back to the homestead with me and stayed for that following week, tending to my needs and desperately trying to get me to eat, but I could not. It was during this period that I got up late one night and went looking for Clement's Colt, only to find it missing from the holster. Hollis had removed it and locked it in the gun cabinet along with every rifle held in that house. Had he not, I would have killed myself in a flash.

When Rita was departing to return to town, she said in passing that my father had ridden over to see me. I didn't think much of it, and Rita said that she had informed him that it was best to leave it for a little while. I expected that he would leave it forever. When he did come to my door it was in the new year of '91. I was still deep in deep mourning and expected that he would briefly offer his condolences and leave. However, that was not the purpose of his visit at all. In fact, he didn't even ask after my well-being or otherwise.

He opened the conversation by saying, 'You'll have a roof over your head, I'll see to that, but not here.'

I didn't know what he was talking about and guessed that I had just misheard what he had said. And, besides, I really couldn't be bothered asking him to repeat it. In fact, I turned to go back inside.

'Did you hear me?' he said. 'You will have a roof over your head, but not here.'

I said, 'Yes, I heard you.' But I didn't understand.

'I'll give you a week to move out, that is only fair.'

I turned back towards him. 'What?'

'A week,' he repeated.

'To move where?'

'Back to where you were brought up. You can live there.'

'Why would I want to go back there? This is my home?'

'Not anymore.'

I was confused. 'What do you mean, not anymore?'

'I own it now,' said my father. 'All of it. It was part of the deal me and Clement did so that he could marry you. We joined our two properties as one. It was a gentleman's agreement. Now that he's gone that leaves me as the sole remaining business partner and owner of both properties. I'll move in here to live, and you can move back to where

40

you lived before. I'll not bother you, and you don't need to bother me.'

I could feel my anger building. 'Get off the Double U now, before I fetch my rifle,' I said. I could feel my whole body shaking with rage.

'I'm going, but remember, you've only got a week, so don't dally.'

'What was that about, Miss Nettie?' asked Hollis as my father was leaving.

'Nothing,' I said, but I knew there was something in it, somewhere, but what?

I spoke to Dutch the next morning and asked if he knew of any arrangement regarding Clement and my father. He said he didn't, but he did suggest that I secure Clement's last will and testament and put it under lock and key, just in case.

I went looking for that will and turned the homestead upside down. Hollis asked what I was doing, and I didn't tell him at first. When I did, he helped but, to no avail. If it existed, we could not find it. Hollis suggested that I go into town and speak to Rita as to what I should do. It was good advice and this I did.

When we spoke, I didn't tell her about my father's visit, just that I couldn't find the will. She immediately suggested that I go over to the Missouri Savings and Loans and speak with Albert Hopkins, as that was the bank where Clement had done business for years, and banks were used to secure important documents. This I did within the same hour, and after Hopkins had pawed my hand with both of his, I asked him straight up if Clement had any important documents secured with the bank. He confirmed that there were several. With relief, I asked, does that include his last will and testament?

'No,' he said slowly, 'I don't believe it does, but let me check.'

41

He disappeared from his office and returned shortly with a long, black, metal box. He lifted the unlocked lid. Inside were a number of folded papers each tied with a ribbon. He went through them one by one, lifting from the box, examining, and telling me of its purpose.

As he laid the last document down, he said, 'Well I'm sorry Mrs Youcheck, all these are just deeds and old loan documents that have now been fully paid. They have been kept only for reference and any future loans. As for a will, or anything else, well as you can see, it is not held by this bank.'

'Is there another tin box with other documents?' I asked.

Albert Hopkins drew in a long breath. 'No, I'm afraid not, this is all there is.'

He was lying.

Oh, how he was lying.

These were not all the documents that were secured in the safe deposit box and held in the bank vault. Some had been removed and one of these was of vital importance to my future. It was the agreement drawn up by Clement and accepted by my father, for the sum of $1,000, that he had no claim on the Double U through kinship from the marriage of his daughter. It had been registered at the bank on the signature of Hopkins and secured. However, he had now removed that document, along with substantial equity in currency and bonds, and tucked them inside his coat pockets for return only after I had left. Will or no will, that one-page document would have put paid to any of my father's plans to seize the Double U from me. But without that knowledge I was now all at sea, in stormy waters, heading for the rocks and without a rudder.

5

HOWEVER

Courtin

I walked out of the Missouri Savings and Loans and into the chill of the morning to feel the frozen air upon my cheeks.

Hollis asked, 'You find that will, Miss Nettie?'

'No,' is all I said.

We drove back over to see Rita. Hollis went inside to pass on the news, while I pondered on what I should do. I was having trouble thinking straight. My brain wouldn't work, and I felt numb all over.

'Nettie.'

I sat staring into the distance, thinking.

'Nettie,' it was Rita, consoling. 'Hollis has just told me.' She was standing by the buggy looking up at me and patting my leg. 'Everything should be all right, lots of men fail to leave a will, but you have your marriage licence. You have legal rights.'

Yes, I thought, of course I do. We were man and wife. We were married for better or worse, for rich or poor, in sickness or in health, till death do us part. I was the lawful wedded wife of Clement Youcheck, and now I was his widow.

'You need to see Lawyer Pruett and let him know that

43

you have not been able to find Clement's will.'

'Do I?'

I didn't know at that time that Rita was a client of Lawyer Pruett. In fact, their relationship in a professional sense was close, because Rita and her girls were constantly under threat of being run out of town by the god-botherers up on the hill, and the odd politician around election time who was chasing sanctimonious votes.

'Always best to have a little legal advice,' said Rita. 'I'll come along with you.'

Lawyer Pruett was genial as he listened to my predicament with his hands clasped below his chin. He also took some notes before saying, 'You have little to worry about Mrs Youcheck. Property law allows you to lay an ownership claim on the Double U through widowhood. However. . . .'

Why do lawyers always have to say, however?

'However, that includes not just the assets but also any liabilities. Are you aware of how your late husband managed the Double U?'

'Yes,' said I with confidence. 'Clement schooled me in the management of the property and stock. Our financial position is sound. My husband was an excellent business-man.'

'Yes, I expected that to be so. However. . . .'

Another, however.

'Are you planning to run the Double U as your husband did?'

'Of course, it is my home,' I said.

'You could sell and live in comfortable surroundings wherever you wished.'

'The Double U is my home,' I repeated.

He nodded. 'Then all I can do is wish you the very best of luck. You deserve it after your tragedy and at such a young age.'

I didn't know what my age had to do with any of this, but I accepted his good wishes.

'Is there anything else?' he asked.

Rita got up, ready to leave, and I was just about to stand when I said, 'Yes, there is something else. My father has made a claim on the Double U.'

Rita sat down with a thump.

Lawyer Pruett reclasped his hands below his chin and asked. 'On what grounds?'

'Grounds?'

'What are his reasons for making such a claim?'

'He said that he had an agreement with Clement that joined both properties, his and ours, as one.'

'Well,' said Lawyer Pruett slowly, 'on the basis of your marriage to Mr Youcheck, and that you are Mr O'Brian's daughter and therefore he was Mr Youcheck's father-in-law, it could be argued, in a way, to be a family arrangement?'

'He didn't say family arrangement,' I said. 'My father said it was a gentleman's agreement.' I then added, 'I'm family and I knew none of this.'

'So, he doesn't have it in writing,' said Lawyer Pruett.

I thought it was a question, so answered, 'That I am unsure of?'

'A gentleman's agreement,' he explained, 'is usually done on a handshake and in good faith, not in writing.' He gazed out of the window, deep in thought, before adding. 'Your husband never discussed any such agreement with you at any time?'

'No, he did not,' I said and sensed that something was wrong, very wrong. I also felt my blood begin to rise.

'What was the relationship like between your father and your husband?'

I knew what he was getting at. 'Are you referring to the gambling debt that got me hitched up?'

Rita coughed, and the Lawyer Pruett wriggled uncomfortably in his seat.

'No need to be embarrassed 'cos I'm not. It is what it was and everyone in the valley knows what happened, but I grew to love that man and he loved me.'

The lawyer looked at Rita then back to me. 'Of that I am sure. But I was referring to the period after you were married. What contact did you and your husband have with your father?'

'None, there was no need. I started a new life and had no need to speak to him.'

'Even out of affection.'

I said nothing.

The lawyer just nodded. 'I see.'

'Can I stay in my home?' I asked, desperate for him to say yes.

He clicked his tongue three times and said slowly, 'Yes,' before pausing again to say, 'However. . . .'

There he went again, another *however*.

'However, what?' I asked abruptly.

'However, your father may challenge for ownership on the basis that there was indeed an agreement.'

'And how would he do that?' asked Rita.

'In court.'

'Court,' repeated Rita. 'If that was to happen, what should Nettie do?'

'Can't say until we see the evidence that is presented, but the question I have for you Mrs Youcheck, is do you think your father *will* challenge?'

'Yes,' came the reply, but it wasn't me, it was from Rita. 'I've known Karl O'Brian before Nettie was born and he will challenge, alright.'

And she was right. Before the last snowfalls of winter had passed, we were in the county court under the title of

O'Brian versus Youcheck. When I heard the case called out by the clerk in the courthouse, I thought it sounded like a tent carnival boxing match, but it was much more serious than just having a few teeth knocked out.

Let me just say that up to this point in time I may not have painted my father in the most flattering light, but I swear upon my heart that I have tried to be faithful in all and every detail of this story. *However* – the word that Lawyer Pruett was so keen to use – that lying, cheating, foul rat of a man would stop at nothing to get his hands on the Double U. And he wanted all of it. He was never going to share it with me or anyone. That it was beyond his abilities to manage such a large property also seemed beyond his comprehension.

In papers brought before the court, my father had signed an affidavit stating that on the shake of a hand an agreement had been made. The substance of this agreement was that on the giving of his blessing for the holy matrimony of his one and only beloved daughter to Clement Youcheck, in return the two properties were co-joined as one and all under the name of the Double U.

My eyes bulged on hearing the words, 'beloved daughter' while Lawyer Pruett quizzed my father on the what, why, when, where and how of this agreement. The vague responses given made it look like his story was starting to fray. Pruett advised the jury, which were all men, that it was common knowledge that the marriage had been initiated through the means of a gambling debt that was owed by my father to Clement. Lawyer Pruett told me and Rita that it was important to tell people what they already knew, to show our open intentions. He went on to tell the jury of how love had blossomed in our relationship and that I had been heartbroken on the loss of my husband.

The jury looked at me with a good degree of sympathy

and I was sure we now had them on our side. But then my father's lawyer, a man named Jefferson – Cornelius Jefferson – said, 'If this was such a lovey-dovey affair, how come Clement Youcheck never wrote out a will that clearly and legally defined the status of ownership of the property to his wife in the event of death?' This was one of those rhetorical questions that learned people love to ask themselves. 'I will tell you why,' he said. 'Because he could not. Clement Youcheck was a man of honour and he knew that he had a business agreement with his father-in-law, who was the joint owner of the Double U.'

Well, when you see twelve heads all bobbing up and down in a small jury box, you know that they are in fierce agreement with what is being proposed to them.

The next day, Lawyer Pruett took a different tack. He asked, 'Mr O'Brian, when you made this verbal agreement with Mr Youcheck to join your two properties, through the marriage of your daughter, were there any witnesses?'

This was not a rhetorical question and I kept my eye on the jury to catch their response when they heard the answer.

'No,' he replied. 'It was just me and him.'

'Did you ever think to advise your daughter of this arrangement?'

'No need,' said my father. 'That was for Youcheck to do. He was about to become her husband. She was now his problem.'

I caught sight of some nodding heads in the jury box.

'Did you ever, by chance, tell anyone of this agreement after it was made, but before Mr Youcheck's untimely death?'

Oh, I thought, we've got you now. Surely, in a place like our valley, where everybody seemed to know everybody else's business, somebody would know, and if they didn't then it wasn't true.

My father was slow in answering. Then after long silence, he said, 'No, I had no need.'

I let out a long sigh of relief.

Then Karl O'Brian said, 'But I know someone who did know about the agreement, but not from me.'

Well, I didn't see that coming and nor did Lawyer Pruett. He was taken aback before he finally asked, 'Who would that be?'

'The manager of the Missouri Savings and Loans Bank, Albert Hopkins,' said my father. 'He told me he knew, when I went to open an account.'

The small courtroom was abuzz with chatter and the judge had to call the court to order.

During the lunchtime adjournment Lawyer Pruett advised me and Rita that he was going to call Hopkins to the stand. Once there, he would get him to testify under oath if he was indeed aware of the agreement, and if so, what were the circumstances of his knowledge.

This was done the following day, first up, but it took some time to get to the vital question, as much old ground had to be covered to put Hopkins in the picture, seeing he had not attended any of the previous proceedings. By nature, Albert Hopkins was a man who liked to be seen as important, and indeed he was. To be on the wrong side of him could easily result in a loan application not being approved. But he and his bank were also reliant on land-holders like Clement. This situation meant that he needed to be respectful, which turned him into a sort of politician both in speech and manner. This was reflected in his answers, none of which were either forthright or clear.

For example, when Lawyer Pruett asked, 'Were you ever advised of an agreement between Mr O'Brian and Mr Youcheck to co-join their two properties?'

Hopkins response was, 'In my profession as manager of banking with the Missouri Savings and Loans in the town of Grange, I am often taken into the confidentialities of business arrangements.'

Well, yeah, we all knew that, I said in my head, but answer the question.

'Quite so,' said Lawyer Pruett. 'And of this particular business arrangement?'

'This one?'

'The one between Mr O'Brian and Mr Youcheck.'

'Regarding?'

'Regarding the joining of the two properties as one.'

'Oh, that?'

'Yes, that?'

'It does make common sense to join the two properties through an alliance of marriage and family. After all, the two holdings share a common boundary on the upper western side of the valley.'

'A small one, but yes, they do,' conceded Lawyer Pruett with courtesy.

I watched all of this and came to the conclusion that this lawyering business seems to be both a patient and well-mannered profession, because Lawyer Pruett did not raise his voice once in frustration, while I was getting most annoyed.

'But putting marriage alliances and geography to one side,' he continued, 'did you, or did you not, have prior knowledge of any agreement between Mr O'Brian and Mr Youcheck?'

'Well, let me see. Knowledge?'

'Yes, did you know of any such agreement? Yes or no?'

'Well—'

Lawyer Pruett interrupted, 'Yes or no?'

'Well, yes,' he said slowly, 'of course I did.'

I felt my stomach churn.

'Can you recall when you were advised?'

'Oh, I'd have to say, quite early in the piece.'

'Before the marriage of Mr Youcheck to Miss O'Brian as she was at that time?'

'Yes.'

'Are you sure?'

'Yes, I am most assuredly sure.'

'Why is that?'

'Well such an arrangement affects the collateral of a property. As the bank manager, I need to know that.'

'But Mr O'Brian didn't tell you?'

'No. Mr O'Brian was not an account holder at that time. But he is now.'

'But not then?'

'No.'

'So, who told you?'

'Why, Clement Youcheck of course.'

Oh, how I wished that Clement could speak to me from his grave to confirm or deny what had just been said under oath, but only silence prevailed upon my ears and it was deafening.

6

DEEP WATER

On My Own

In the pandemonium that followed the revelation by
Albert Hopkins that Clement had told him of an arrangement that joined both properties, I saw the look on the
jurors' faces as they fixed their eyes upon my father. I had
seen those same looks given to Clement when we went to
town together. It is the gaze of the common man when he
holds someone to be above him in terms of importance or
wealth. In this case it was wealth. They now saw my father
in this new appealing light. He was now the owner of the
Double U, and had instantly become wealthy and therefore someone of substance and worth knowing. It is the
secret dream of every man to strike it rich, and I now
knew, in a heartbeat, in whose favour the jury were going
to decide.

From this turning point there was little more that
Lawyer Pruett could do but fight a rearguard action and try

to secure my place as an equal co-owner of the Double U, while I sat and watched the administration of the law unfold; twelve neighbours could take away from me half of my marriage entitlement on no more than a verbal agreement, with no witnesses and on the word of just two men. That one of those men was my husband's banker, and the other my father, left me both bewildered and dumbstruck. Surely, it couldn't get any worse? But how wrong you can be in a storm. When cussing your bad luck for having a leak in the ceiling, off blows the roof!

My co-ownership with my father should have accommodated the legal custody of half of all property and assets, and more importantly given me an equal say in how both joint properties were to be managed. Not that I was much interested in the piddling place that was our family farm – it was the Double U that was the grand prize. But my father and Lawyer Cornelius Jefferson had not finished with me just yet.

It was put to the court that as I was so young, not yet twenty years of age, that it would be prudent for all matters of management and business to be vested in my father, until I turned twenty-one. And I guess a reasonable man would say that sounds, well, reasonable. After all, nineteen years is young when viewed through the eyes of old men in a jury box, and besides, my twenty-first birthday was less than eighteen months away, so it was not a long wait. Accordingly, the twelve reasonable men of the jury agreed with the proposition, and the judge said, 'Let it be so.'

There was, of course, another reason for the acceptance of this proposal. I was a woman – and one that they saw as merely a slip of a girl, because that's how it was back then. It was to take many, many years before anything much changed in regard to a woman's place in the greater scheme of the world, but this is not the time nor place to address such matters, as curious as they are.

What went through my mind immediately on hearing this court decree was the damage my father could do to the Double U in a year and a half. Not only was he lacking in skills to manage such a large holding, with its stock cycles and permanent and itinerant workforce, but he was also a weak-minded man who would take without giving back. I had seen it first-hand all my life. There was also the terrible niggling thought that he could drain all the cash from the accounts, sell off assets, and not put back the planned capital to grow or even maintain the land, the stock or the buildings. His own property had never prospered over the twenty years he had supposedly worked that land. His approach was akin to subsistence farming and, even then I used to go hungry from time to time to feed my father first. Yet it could have been much more. It was in the best part of the valley and protected from extreme weather by the terrain and vegetation. It was well drained in winter and water was retained in the spring over the hottest of summers. It could thrive in the hands of a diligent owner.

I left the courthouse defeated and returned to the Double U, where I packed up my personal belongs. As I was leaving the master bedroom, I caught a glimpse of myself in the big mirror and remembered when I had stood looking at myself with Clement standing behind, his big arms wrapped around me tight. 'Oh, Clem,' I said to the image, 'I've lost you, I've lost the Double U, and now I'm lost without you,' and burst into tears.

I suppose I could have tried to negotiate with my father to stay, but what for? What he had done to me was deeply personal and I didn't want to be anywhere near him, and certainly not under the same roof. So, I moved back to the property where I had grown up.

It was Hollis who once again came to my aid and loaded

up the buckboard for the trip. The last thing he placed on board was the old rocking chair from the front room, saying that it had belonged to Clement's mother, Gerty, and her mother, Muscha before that. He said I should have it with me, as it belonged to the ladies of the Double U. But just as we were about to leave, my father called to Hollis to take it down and put it back. He went to protest until I put my hand on his arm and shook my head.

'Put it on the porch,' said my father to Hollis. 'You can put it back inside when you return.'

Hollis straightened his back, lifting his frame to its full height. 'I won't be returning,' he said. 'I work for Miss Nettie, not you.' It was said with defiance.

'I have no money to pay you, Hollis,' I said quietly, 'you need to stay and keep your job.'

'No,' he said back under his breath. 'He may be your father but I ain't working for that man. You and me will work something out and we will do it together, just as we done before.'

Such loyalty is rare in this life and I have drawn the conclusion that it is a mark of a person's character and a form of sincere and deep love. Now, I'm not talking about physical love or anything like that, but the love that should be the bond within every family. And from that moment Hollis became my family. The Lord had delivered a saint in my hour of need. And boy did I need it.

I can't tell you of the cold, black, vacant feeling that swept over me when the buckboard pulled up at the old farmhouse where I had grown up. It was never a place of fond memories to begin with, but now it took on a new and ominous position in my life. I was like a captive returning to prison for a crime I did not commit. For the first week I could hardly bring myself to rise from my bed. Hollis didn't scold or even cajole me to get up. He seemed to know that this phase would pass in its own good time, and it did. Every indulgence has its limits and even my weak and feeble mind knew that a week in bed was way too long. Besides, Clement was close at hand by constantly being in my thoughts and dreams, and he said to me. 'Enough is enough, girl. Time to get up and contribute.' So, I got up and tried to function as best I could.

Now melancholia has many names. The negro calls it the blues. The Irish call it the black dog. I called it my heavy heart. But it is all one and the same – it is the wretchedness of despair and the desolation of the soul. When you have it, and I had it bad, you believe that you will never be light of heart again. However, all things must eventually pass to some degree or other. Sure, it never truly disappears as I can still get weepy remembering my Clem, especially on birthdays and anniversaries, and it will never change. I'm an old gal now, close to eighty and prone to sentimentality when thinking of the past. It is all I have left. But for those next six months I was in misery, yet little by little, the burden started to lift.

My first recollection that I was on the mend was when I was sitting on the front porch bench late that summer while seeking a breeze. Hollis was sitting down on the step humming quietly as he fixed a hole in one of his shoes.

When he stopped I asked, 'What's that tune?'

'Oh, it was just something that my momma would sing when I was bitty.'

'Does it have a name?'

'Deep River.'

'Pretty,' I said.

'The tune is pretty, but the feelin's not.'

'Why?'

'Oh, it's an old slave song and it's about crossing over.'

'The river?' I asked.

He looked away. 'Yeah, something like that?'

But it wasn't. I thought about it later that night and it dawned on me that it was about death. In the slave song I guess it was better to be dead and with Jesus than a slave on a cotton plantation and under the thumb of a white owner, and I could appreciate that. I would rather be dead and with Clement than a slave to my father. Both Hollis and me just wanted a little freedom to live life on our own terms. Fortunately, I had Hollis to assist me, while I guess he had his faith in the Lord. I wished that I had his faith, but I hadn't been blessed in the belief of the kingdom across that river.

The following evening, I asked, 'Hollis, was your mammy a slave?' I knew the answer.

Hollis nodded.

'Your father?'

'Same.'

'And you?'

'I was born that way then got the emancipation after the war. I was a man then, but younger. Still, I'd never known no other life, it was too late for me.'

I knew all that, too. But I was building to my big question. 'Hollis, do you feel free now?'

He said nothing, He didn't need to. I had my answer. 'I don't,' I said. 'Never have, except for my time at the Double U when I was with Clement and you.'

'With me,' said Hollis, surprised. 'I didn't have nothing to do with you feeling emancipated. That was you and Mister Clement.'

'Oh, yes you did, and you know it in your heart. You are the pappy I never had.'

'Don't you go saying such things.'

'I just did.'

'Well don't go repeating them, out loud.'

'Only to you?'

'Not even me.'

'Why not?'

'You'll get us both in trouble.'

'Maybe trouble is needed to be truly emancipated.'

Hollis was shaking his head. 'You and me, we will never be truly emancipated.'

'Why?'

'You is a woman and I am black, or haven't you noticed either?'

'Well, maybe I should keep turning a blind eye to both.'

'Then you'll be truly blind in both eyes.'

'Probably,' I said, 'and in deep water.'

And that is where the seed came from. It was just a casual conversation that got me thinking. What do I have to do to free myself of this situation and get back total control of the Double U? And I mean, get all of it back in my own name, and if necessary by hook or by crook.

7

A STING

The Answer Is Work

This was my turning point. It allowed me to swing my thoughts from the past to the present, and then to the future. It gave me a purpose. I would work out how I, Nettie Youcheck, an almost twenty-year-old widow, stripped of her rightful inheritance and banished, could reverse such bad fortune. I was going to swim the deep water and I was going to cross that river to stand upon that other side, sanctified.

But where to start?

I turned to the scriptures. Not for prayer but for inspiration as my situation seemed not unlike a biblical tale. I looked to those stories where good had claimed victory over evil, especially where the odds were not on the side of the weak. I found my old Sunday school book and went a'reading. I always liked the story of Daniel in the lions' den, but it offered nothing other than a feeling of being caged up. There was the story of Elijah being fed by the ravens, but not much there either. Nor from Noah, unless there was to be a flood in our valley that was going to sweep my father away. Sodom and Gomorrah held my interest because I felt as one with Lot's wife – I too would have looked back, just out of curiosity. Why not? Who gets to see mayhem every day? What about Samson and Delilah? Could I be a Delilah, I thought? I was running out of stories, so I went to the New Testament, only to find even less education.

Hollis saw what I was doing and quizzed me. 'You got religion all of sudden?'

I had to come clean. 'No. I am looking for stories of redemption.'

'Redemption from what?'

'From our pitiful state.'

'Which is?'

'Cast upon this barren farm.' I thought the biblical connection was smart, but not for long.

Hollis responded by saying, 'I would think you need a book on farming, not a bible book. Your husband had plenty of farming books. He had books on the use of ploughs, care of livestock, and planting of crops. They are all in the big bookcase over at the Double U.'

'They could be handy,' I agreed.

Hollis nodded in confirmation. 'We could make a go of this property. All we need is a little capital to buy the right implements and seed.'

'I was thinking of more direct ways of redemption,' I announced.

Hollis gave me one of his famous looks where he tilts his head back ever so slightly and narrowed his eyes. 'More direct ways of redemption,' he repeated back to me.

'Yes,' I said.

'Like what in particular?'

'Oh, I was thinking of taking back what is rightfully mine.'

'How exactly?'

'Don't know, exactly, that's why I'm doing some reading.' I got the feeling that Hollis wasn't convinced by my approach. 'I was just seeing if there was something in the scriptures that gave clarity on how the weak. . . .' I was searching for the right words.

'Will inherit the earth?' he said slowly.

'Yes, just like that.'

'You've already inherited the earth. It's called the Double U.'

'I've lost half of it and have no say over the half I have been left with until I am twenty-one.' Then I added for good measure. 'We have lost our home.' I was trying to draw Hollis into my plot with the mention to 'our home'. However, I may have been laying it on a bit thick judging from Hollis's slanty eyed look. 'And I mean to get it back, all of it.'

'And how are you going to do that?'

'By a-looking.'

'Looking in bible stories?'

'Why not? There are lots of stories in the bible of inheriting back.'

'Must have missed those ones, 'cos I've only seen the taking back ones.'

'Same thing isn't it?'

'Don't think so,' said Hollis shaking his head. 'One is receiving, and one is getting. Do you know what I think you are talking about? I think you are talking about taking back by the use of might.'

I poked my chin out. 'If necessary. Might can be right.'

'Depends who's doing the mightering. What *might* do you have?'

'I have you.'

'I rest my case,' said Hollis. 'You have no forces.'

'I have my brains.'

'Yes, I will grant you that. But are you as smart as David when he was up against Goliath?'

'That's the one I was looking for,' I said with glee.

'Oh, that was the one? So, you are planning on hitting your own daddy in the eye with a rock from a slingshot?'

'If I thought it would work, I would.'

'David killed Goliath, then cut off his head. You wouldn't do that to your own father, would you?'

My mind began to spin. If my father were to die, I would inherit back the half he had taken. These thoughts must have been written all over my face.

'Are you having dangerous thoughts, Miss Nettie? Because, I think it best you stop right now and we concentrate on building up this farm, first.'

'Then what?'

'Then you show that you are a good farmer and are able to have a say in the running of the Double U once you turn of age. We need to put in more vegetables, get some hogs, and get strong fruit on our trees; and all before you turn twenty-one in just a year.'

'The Double U is more than a few vegetables, hogs and fruit. It is about raising cattle and grazing and corn,' I said.

'Sure, and we can do a little of that. All we need is the capital.'

'And where are we going to get that?'

'Go and ask your daddy.'

'I'll never do that.' I was strident in my response.

'Is that pride talking?'

I didn't answer.

'Then you'll need to get the money from the bank,' said Hollis.

'I have no say over the getting of money from the bank accounts. The court fixed that.'

'You can still ask for a loan from the bank. Everybody borrows from the bank, black and white. It's what poor people do, and you is poor, at the moment.'

'How do I pay back the borrowings?'

'We can plant more than we need and sell to market. And you only have to keep up the payments till you turn twenty-one. Then you can draw from the Double U accounts and pay back the rest. Mr Hopkins was always bowing his head to your husband and he will want to keep on your good side, for when you turn twenty-one.'

I couldn't fault what Hollis was saying. 'I'm being persuaded,' I said. 'It must be the voice of experience talking?'

Hollis nodded. 'I'm way, way older than you Miss Nettie and if there is one thing that I've learnt over the years it's the power of hard work. What you work for in this life, you get to keep. That is America.'

There was a sting in the tail of Hollis's words. I had never worked to own any part of the Double U. I would have in time, if Clement had lived, but we were only together for just over one year. My contribution had been small. Hollis was right; I needed to work and prove my worth to one and all, that I was capable of operating the Double U.

8

CAPITAL

Cash is King

My return visit to see Mr Albert Hopkins at the Missouri
Savings and Loans held no trepidation. Why should it?
First, his bank had previously provided loans to the Double
U, so why not one to me. Second, I just took for granted
that he had truthfully shown me all the contents of the safe
deposit box and that he was sympathetic to my plight. As
for the evidence he'd given in court, yes it certainly crossed
my mind as more than a little odd that Clement would
enter into *any* agreement with my father and not tell me,
but Hopkins had given his evidence under oath, so it had
to be true. Albert Hopkins was an important man in our
community with both responsibilities and authority and
therefore demanded respect.

What I didn't know at that point in time was that he was
a dirty, devious liar, who had personally hidden from me an
important document that would remove any claim by my
father over the Double U. This was a man who had also
entered into an arrangement with my father to make a
known false statement that Clement had entered into a

64

verbal agreement to join the two properties. In fact, my husband had done all in his power to prevent such an event from ever occurring. Without knowing it, I was like Daniel in the lion's den, and it was Hopkins who had put me there, to be eaten up.

Of course, not knowing any of this at that particular time, I believed that Hollis was right. Stay on the straight and narrow, work hard and inherit the earth. In just over a year I would be able to have a say in the management of the Double U. Now was the time to show that I knew how to make a property profitable – something my father could never do.

In my naive way, I also believed that I would have the law on my side to help with any grievances or discord I may have with my father, once I became the legitimate half owner of the Double U. I therefore felt sure that I would be well received by the manager of the Missouri Savings and Loans, and that my case for borrowing capital would be favourably received and given all due consideration.

I prepared, on paper, a summary of the items and goods needed and measured each of these against the costs of purchase from either the general store or the stock agent. I had originally thought that a loan of four hundred dollars would cover all requirements. However, Hollis suggested that I factor in a price rise, saying, 'You know that prices rise each and every year. Costs are always going up, never down. You don't want to be surprised next season when you don't have enough money to pay for what you need.'

With this adjustment, I realized that I would therefore need close to four hundred and fifty dollars. Finally, I decided to ask for a loan of four hundred and eighty-five dollars, which would leave me some room to reduce that amount during any negotiations, if necessary, to show prudence.

Before my marriage, such an amount would have seemed like treasure, but my time at the Double U had exposed me to the costs and capital required. Clement had previously borrowed in the tens of thousands of dollars, mine was small and measured in the hundreds, but it would set me apart from my youth as Nettie O'Brian the housekeeper, and mark me as Nettie Youcheck the businesswoman.

I didn't make an appointment to see Manager Hopkins. Clement never made any appointments when he went into town. He would just turn up and people would be happy to see him at any time of the day. Hollis dusted down the old buckboard and placed a folded grain sack upon the bench seat where I sat. I had become accustomed to the cushioning of the leather seat on the buggy, but that now belonged to my father.

A clerk by the name of Alex Milton greeted me when I arrived at the bank counter and he knew me by both sight and name. I had no recollection of ever being introduced, however I was careful to excuse myself for not remembering him. He pleasantly confirmed that we had never formally met, but that he had seen me with my departed husband whom he had admired. I accepted his civility and took up a seat upon the pew near the standing clock, as he departed to instruct the manager of my presence.

I waited for some time before the clerk returned to advise that the manager was busy and unable to see me. I sensed that Mr Milton, who was not much older than myself, was somewhat embarrassed by this state of affairs. I said, no matter, I could return within the hour. He looked uneasy, which suggested that I should leave it longer.

'When then?' I asked.

'The manager is very busy.'

'I'm sure he is, but this won't take long, I've come prepared,' I said. 'Just give me a time to return.' I looked at the clock. It was just after one.

'Four o'clock,' he said tentatively.

I was annoyed but said, 'Very well, four o'clock.'

The three-hour wait was an inconvenience. I had no other business to attend to in town, yet it did not provide sufficient time to return home as the duration by buckboard was the best part of an hour. No sooner would we arrive, before having to start back again. Hollis suggested that we go down near the creek and water the horses near the arrow-woods, which we did, returning on the dot of four, after three frustrating hours of lost time.

On return, Alex Milton approached me and I could see that he was agitated.

'I'm sorry, Mrs Youcheck,' he said. 'Mr Hopkins has had to leave for the day.' Then he added. 'Unexpectedly.'

'When will he be back?' I asked.

'Not sure.'

'But not back today?' I asked.

'No, I don't think so,' said the bank clerk.

'So, when should I return?'

'I really don't know.'

'Tomorrow, the day after, or the day after that?'

'I really can't say.'

'Please, tell Mr Hopkins that I will be back on Thursday. That gives him three days to make some time available for me. I will need no more than half an hour as I only wish to draw up documents for a loan of four hundred and eighty-five dollars.'

'Yes,' said the clerk. 'I will pass that on.' But his voice was that of an uncertain man, and that annoyed me.

I turned and left without a by your leave to express my displeasure at being shown so little respect. I had not expected to be treated this way. I had been given the brush-off. Hopkins, clearly, did not see me as a priority in his daily schedule. So much so that he couldn't even give me a personal explanation. Had Clement been alive it would have been different. I had seen Hopkins snivel in my husband's presence.

On Wednesday afternoon Rita came to visit unexpectedly. Several months had passed since our last meeting and I had not been good company. On seeing her at my door, I immediately felt guilty for not having visited her on the Monday when I'd been in town. I had no excuse as I had sat idly down by creek for three hours.

'I'm going to town tomorrow. I planned to call.' It was a fib. In truth, I had become a recluse and found it difficult to see anyone who reminded me of my time with Clement or at the Double U.

'I know,' she said.

'You knew I was coming to visit you tomorrow?' I said a little too surprised.

'No,' said Rita. 'I just knew that you were coming to town to see Hopkins.'

'You did?'

'Alex Milton told me.'

'Oh,' I said.

'He was agitated.'

I dropped my eyes. 'Has he asked for an apology?'

Rita looked puzzled. 'Apology for what?'

'I was rude to him. I left in a mood. Hopkins wasn't available to see me, and when I returned later, after waiting, he had gone for the day. It wasn't Mr Milton's fault. He was only the messenger. But I was in a temper.'

'No, Alex didn't mention any of that. He came to talk to me about other matters.'

'Other matters, concerning me?'

Rita was not her unruffled self. 'He won't see you, Nettie.'

Now I was puzzled. Confused even. 'Mr Milton won't see me?' I asked.

'No. Albert Hopkins won't see you.'

'Why?'

Rita paused as if not wanting to say.

'Why not?' I asked again.

'I believe that he is in cahoots with your father.'

'How exactly?'

'Through banking arrangements.'

I didn't know what Rita was getting at. Of course, my father would be connected to Hopkins through banking arrangements. After all, he had taken over the Double U and was now the lawful authority over all the bank accounts, and they were held at the Missouri Savings and Loans.

'I just want a loan, that's all,' I explained. 'To build up this property and show that I have the ability to run the Double U.'

Rita bit at her bottom lip and her eyes became glassy. 'Oh Nettie, Nettie, you will never be allowed to run the Double U.'

'Why not?' I blurted. 'The law says, when I'm twenty-one.'

'Don't depend on the law, Nettie. The Double U has been taken from you.' Then Rita said, 'in all but name.'

'They can't.' I was getting heated.

'According to Alex, it has already happened.'

How could this be, I asked myself, as I felt my anger rise to the point where some of those seething sentiments splashed onto Rita when I shouted. 'How do you know this? Why have you come to make mischief and stomp on my dreams of managing the Double U in my own right.'

Rita clutched me by the shoulders and dragged me into her arms to press me against her bosom. 'Shush, shush, shush, child,' she said. 'I would never trample on your dreams, Nettie. I've just come to warn you.'

I had not been held and hugged for so long, and I had certainly never been embraced in such a way by another woman. It was warm, it was loving, and it was motherly. Rita had come out of concern, for me, and in return I had hissed and spat at her like a wild cat. I felt so ashamed and burst into tears. 'What am I going to do, Rita? I need the Double U back, all of it. It is my home. You understand, don't you?'

Rita was patting my back in comfort. 'Yes, I do child,' she said.

I lifted my head and pleaded. 'So, what am I to do?'

Rita looked down on me and I could see the tracks of her tears. 'I don't know, Nettie, I just don't know.'

9

SECRETS

And Lies

I will now provide you with a rundown of events and confidences that led Rita to my door with her warning, as it will help to fill in the background.

On finally gathering a little composure, I invited Rita inside to sit with me. This she did, still affording me comfort, while Hollis put on the coffee pot. To say that I asked a series of insightful questions to establish the facts of the matter is far from the truth. My head was still spinning fast and my queries were not only all over the place but garbled and stumbled over. Rita sat, listened, then spoke clearly as she explained; yet when she left I remained confused in my twirling head. It was only a day or two later and through constant ruminating that the fuzzy picture became clear. So, it is best that I bypass my process from confusion to clarity by just telling you of my conclusions. This means that I need to start at the beginning, well before I walked into the bank to see Albert Hopkins with the view to securing a loan.

Alex Milton, the bank clerk at the Missouri Savings and

Loans, plays an important part, so you need to know about this young man. He had come to Grange from Philadelphia two years prior. His was a planned journey to the West and one that was hoped to make him a self-reliant man, who would then return to city life and the business of commerce. His father's influence had secured the job with the bank at Grange, which was to be for a tenure of one year. Alex was well educated, having attended Girard College where he shone, particularly in the ways of arithmetic and algebra. However, his schooling had not left the mark of a man. He was still a boy in many ways. Rita said that while he was polite and respectful, he was way too eager to please, which she saw as a softness. She therefore predicted that he wouldn't last the distance in a tough town like Grange, but he did.

I asked, 'Why is he still here after two years? Surely he would prefer to return to a softer life?'

'That's precisely what I thought, too,' said Rita. 'He surprised me. He has taken to the ways of the West and grown up. Another city boy who has fallen in love with wide open spaces.' Then she added, 'and our Hazel.'

Alex, I was told, was terribly shy around women. Rita had noticed it immediately on meeting him on a visit to the bank, just after he had arrived and taken up his appointment. Not long after, when Rita was in the general store with one of her girls – the one named Hazel – she caught Alex talking to himself behind the fabric display. She thought that he may have needed some friendly assistance and on approaching him from the side she observed his nervous disposition, which had manifested as large red welts on his neck, as he rehearsed his lines to reintroduce himself to Rita.

'I'm here,' said Rita, 'so just say, hello.'

The poor boy jumped in the air and his face turned

bright red with embarrassment as his eyes darted back and forth, and Rita realized that it was Hazel whom he wanted to meet. She waved the young woman over, introduced her to Alex and suggested that he might like to call the following Sunday and take her for a picnic down by the creek. This he did, all fumbles and stutters with a lunch basket in hand and a bunch of white ox-eyed daisies. By evening a romance had bloomed.

On hearing of this matter some little time later, Albert Hopkins addressed Alex and told him that all of Rita's girls were unsuitable and to end the sordid arrangement immediately, or he would advise his father personally in writing.

'Poor Alex,' said Rita. 'He was distressed to the point of tears and sought my counsel.' She tried all the usual ploys – other fish in the sea, one day he would find a nice girl back in Philly, and that the love of a young man is always transitory. But she could not dissuade him, so she gently spoke to him about Hazel's professional life. Yet none of her urgings as much as budged him one inch. He was not just smitten but deeply in love. This led Rita to go against an age-long principle that she had stuck to all her life and served her well. She got involved and intervened on his behalf. She went and saw Albert Hopkins to convince him to turn a blind eye.

At the time I never asked how she managed to perform such a feat, but I did later. Her reply was simple, 'Secrets.'

I then asked, 'What secrets?'

'Everyone in the valley has a secret,' she said, 'and I know most of them. How do you think I've been able to survive all these years when each town mayoral candidate at election time runs on a ticket of law and order to clean up Grange of immoral inconveniences?'

'So, what was Hopkins' secret?' I asked.

Rita would not be specific other than to say that it was

not that far removed from Alex's dalliance and involved some kind of dressing up. I guessed it was like me pretending to be Annie Oakley and suggested that maybe he wanted to be just like Buffalo Bill. Rita just rolled her eyes and said something about wearing rouge, which I interpreted to mean that he preferred to look like a red Indian. Not sure why he would want to do such a thing, but hey, each to his own.

Although Rita had saved the day, to which Alex was eternally grateful, Hopkins made it known to the young bank clerk that he was most unhappy with having his authority questioned. In fact, as manager, he made this known via his frostiness towards the young man. Yet Alex Milton got on about his work in a congenial fashion. Although he did tell Rita that had it not been for the pleasantry of the bank customers, who he dealt with daily, he would have left. One of those customers was Clement, who Alex soon came to admire, and of course, his face lit up every time Rita arrived to deposit the previous day's takings from her business.

It was Alex who had noted a deposit discrepancy in Rita's account and brought it to Hopkins attention. The manager was dismissive, saying it was no more than a paper error. However, this left Rita's account short to the tune of one hundred dollars, while this same sum was additional to the audited amount in the cash box in the bank vault. This meant that anyone with access could take the money, put it in their pocket and leave without any repercussions as Rita's account and the cash account had been reconciled. And that's precisely what Alex did. He took the money and returned it to Rita, explaining what had occurred.

While Rita was grateful of such an act of unexpected loyalty, she was fearful of the consequences for Alex and told him to put it back immediately. The poor bank clerk was crushed. He had expected appreciation. Instead, he felt like he'd been scolded.

'No, you don't understand,' said Rita. 'It is worth that amount alone to know that Albert Hopkins is cheating me. And it is worth another one hundred to have him totally unaware of my knowledge.'

Alex still thought that he had failed, so Rita added, 'And it is worth much, much more to have you protecting my interests.'

The young man responded with a bright smile. 'Really?' he said.

Rita nodded and conferred on him the status of a close ally. 'Just keep your eye on Mr Albert Hopkins for me and let me know if anything else is untoward.'

'Like what?' asked Alex.

'Let me be the judge of that. Just let me know when Hopkins behaves less like a bank manager should in the discharge of his duties.'

Alex agreed and returned the money without anyone knowing what he had done, other than himself and Rita.

When Alex saw the way I had been treated by Hopkins on my visit to secure a loan, he had confided in Rita not only of the events, but that Hopkins had not left the bank that day. He also told Rita that Hopkins had ordered him to lie to me regarding his whereabouts. This, he said, had fallen heavy upon his conscience and asked what he should do?

Rita said that before she offered any advice, she needed to know why Hopkins wished to avoid meeting with me for something as innocent as a bank loan. She carefully quizzed Alex on every aspect of the accounts of the Double U, going right back to before Clement's death.

'The Double U is the most lucrative of all accounts. It is worth a fortune in capital, collateral, cash and fees to the bank,' said Alex before adding, 'Or it was.'

The *or it was* comment rang in Rita's ears like a fire bell.

Alex explained that after the death of Clement, Hopkins had placed a caveat on the Double U accounts advising that he wanted to know immediately of all withdrawals and if anyone came calling to view the contents of the safe deposit box.

'Why?' asked Rita.

'The rumour in the bank was that expenditure remained high, but there was little income from the sale of livestock or corn, so the main account was starting to drain. There was also a rumour that Karl O'Brian was drinking heavily.'

Rita gave a knowing smirk as if to confirm Alex's last remark before asking, 'Have you ever seen what's in the safe deposit box?'

'I have,' said Alex, 'but only in the presence of Mr Youcheck, so I haven't seen any of the contents since his death.'

'Can you recall what was in it?'

'No, not in detail,' he replied. 'It just seemed to be the usual banking and security documents relating to current stocks and bonds, as well as past loans. Mr Youcheck did place cash in the box from time to time, especially after the sale of cattle on market day.'

'You don't remember if there was a last will and testament in the box, do you?'

Alex shook his head slowly. 'No, I can't recall such a document.'

'Pity. If only we knew for sure. It would be such a vital document to the fortunes of Mrs Youcheck.'

'Even if there was a will in the box, I wouldn't be able to get it on my own, anyway,' said Alex.

'No, I don't want you to take anything, but just knowing if it existed would have been more than helpful.'

'I can still tell you that,' brightened up Alex.

'Really? How?'

'I'll look in the contents register.'

'What's the contents register?' quizzed Rita.

'It is a ledger dating back to the establishment of the Grange Branch. It records everything held in the vault. Every bank has one and each bank deposit box has a separate page that lists all the contents held. When a box is opened the contents are checked against the register. This mostly occurs when the owner of the deposit box is present, but also during the annual audit.'

'Do you have access to this register?'

'Yes, I'm in the vault almost every day.'

'Would it be possible for me to see that register?'

'No,' said Alex. 'It never leaves the vault, and a customer must be escorted into the vault by Mr Mummery, the chief clerk. I don't have the seniority to act as an escort.'

'Is a bank customer with a safe deposit box able to see the register?'

'Only the page that lists the contents of their safe deposit box,' explained Alex. 'It is a requirement of banking confidentiality. A ribbon is used to mark the page so that the register is only opened for that particular box and no other.'

'Damn,' said Rita under her breath.

'But I can look at the register for you and see if the contents list a will.'

'When?' Rita asked excitedly.

'Tomorrow, I guess.'

'Do it, Alex. I need to know, but please be careful.'

'You think that something is being hidden from Mrs Youcheck, don't you?'

'I suspect so.' And with that, she leant across and kissed Alex gently on the cheek and said, 'Thank you, Alex. You are indeed a friend to me and Nettie.'

10

THE DOCUMENT

In The Box

'Rita, tell me, what did Mr Milton find out?' I was impatient.

Rita was apprehensive. 'Nettie, we all need to be very careful. Alex has put himself at great risk for me and I must protect him, and in turn you must protect me. What I am going to tell you will require a cool head. You must promise me that you will stay calm and not do anything without my knowledge.'

I noticed her apprehension as I nodded my agreement, but my silent response didn't seem to cut it with Rita. 'No, Nettie, I mean it. I have given much thought to this visit. My instincts told me to say nothing, but I owe it to Clement. He and I went back a long way. And I also owe it to you.'

'Why me?' I asked and nearly said *we hardly go back any way.* But I was aware of the fondness that Rita held for me. I just didn't fully understand why.

'Because your mother and I were once close, very close.

I knew her even before I met Clement. Right back to a time when Grange was a rough town, especially for pretty young things.'

I nodded my head slowly in agreement again. 'I think I understand,' I said. 'You are going to tell me something that might spark a reaction.'

Years later, Rita would retell this story over a glass of champagne or two, and I must admit I always loved hearing it. 'Might spark a reaction!' she would shriek. 'Spark a reaction. What I told you was dynamite.' And it was true, what she was to tell me was the same as lighting a fuse to a powder keg.

Alex Milton had returned to Rita the following evening to report.

'You saw the register?' she asked.

'I did.'

'And?'

'No will.'

'Oh,' said Rita, who had convinced herself that a will did exist and that it was in the safety deposit box held at the bank. 'Definitely no will?' she quizzed.

'Definitely.'

'Then what are the contents?'

'The register lists railroad bonds along with fifty thousand dollars in cash.'

'Fifty thousand in cash?'

'Yes,' confirmed Alex. 'Mr Youcheck often retained cash from cattle sales for the purchase of breeding stock or unforeseen expenses.'

This surprised Rita, who threw her head back and inadvertently exclaimed, 'Holy shit,' before noticing the mortification on Alex's face. 'Sorry Alex, but get used to it, women cuss, though not usually in a man's company, unless they like them a lot.'

This explanation seemed to leave a favourable impression on the young bank clerk as he pulled his chair in a little closer to Rita and said, lowering his voice, 'Mrs Youcheck could have used some of that money, couldn't she?'

'You've taken the words from my mouth,' said Rita. 'And that bastard Albert Hopkins wouldn't even accommodate Nettie for a loan. What a sh—' She cut the word short, mindful that her language was becoming very unladylike.

Alex made a small cough to hide any embarrassment. 'Do you want me to list the rest of the contents in the security box?'

'Yes, of course.'

'As I said, no will or testament has ever been listed as one of the documents. The register lists a number of loan documents that have since been discharged. These are usually kept for reference should new loans be raised.'

Rita was getting a little impatient. 'Anything else?'

'A number of title documents,' Alex lowered the tone of his speaking voice to display a sense of knowledge and authority. 'These are important as they relate to the purchase of additional land over the years and securing them is wise.'

Rita was dismissive. 'What else?'

'Just one other document is registered. It is an agreement between Mr Youcheck and Mr O'Brian.'

Rita felt her heart sink. 'That must be the agreement to join the two properties.' It was said with resignation.

'That's what I thought too, at first,' said Alex.

'But it wasn't?' questioned Rita.

'It can't be. That was supposed to be a gentleman's agreement, remember? It was verbal, not a written record. And there were no witnesses at the time and place when it was made.'

'Yes,' said Rita, impressed. 'That's right. Your memory serves you well.'

'When it was reported in the Grange Chronicle during the trial, it was of much discussion at the bank as it involved the transfer of property and assets between two customers.'

'So, what could be the content of this agreement between Mr Youcheck and Mr O'Brian?' asked Rita.

'I had no idea, that's why I went and took a look.'

'You opened the box?'

Alex gave a grin. 'Accidentally on purpose.'

Rita was confused. 'Accidentally on purpose when?'

'Today.'

Rita jumped to her feet on hearing this and said quickly, 'Go on.'

'Each day at least three or four boxes are opened for customers. So, when Mr Mummery asked me to get Mrs Hatshaw's deposit box, I accidently on purpose collected the wrong box and key and took it to him at his desk. On opening it, Mr Mummery immediately realized that it was the wrong box. I apologised for the mistake and returned it to the vault to collect the right box. But Mr Youcheck's box had not been locked by Mr Mummery, that was left for me to do and this gave me the briefest of opportunities, while on my own in the vault, to take a look.'

'And what did you find?'

'The document is just one page made out by Mr Youcheck in his hand and signed by Mr O'Brian's mark.'

'Saying?'

'That Mr O'Brian could never make a claim on the Double U under any circumstances, as he had been remunerated in full, to the sum of $1,000, for the release of his daughter's hand to marry.'

Rita swayed a little on her feet like a tree in the wind before she fell back into her chair with a thud. 'I don't know what to say,' she said, shaking her head in astonishment.

'What about holy shit?' offered Alex.

'That's not enough, so don't tempt me.' Rita drew in two or three long breaths, before saying, 'And a young man of your tender years should not be using such language. When you're older like me, then on occasion, it's permissible.'

'What about a little cussing in the company of people I like a lot.'

Rita smiled and extended her hand, and as Alex took it, her fingers squeezed with affection. 'Then it's permissible,' she said, before asking. 'You didn't take it and bring it with you, did you?'

'Oh, no,' said the young bank clerk. 'I learnt my lesson after taking the money from the vault and bringing it here to you.'

'Pity,' said Rita, 'if the sheriff or Lawyer Pruett was to see it and take it to the judge, then Nettie would have the Double U back.'

Alex looked anxious. 'That would make life complicated. At least for me.'

Rita could see that Alex was concerned. 'How?'

'My actions to date are enough to have my employment terminated. But to take a registered document, unauthorised, from the bank and give it to a third party is worse than stealing. No matter what the circumstances, I would never be able to work in banking again.'

'Of course,' said Rita.

'Then there is the other issue.'

'Other issue?'

'Yes. The ledger records that the last time the box was opened officially was by our manager in the presence of Mrs Youcheck. Had she been presented with that document as part of the contents of the safe deposit box, then as you say, this whole affair of her sole ownership would be resolved. It is clear that Albert Hopkins has deceived Mrs Youcheck, lied under oath, and is in cahoots with Mr O'Brian.'

Rita started to see the repercussions related to the knowledge of this secret. She knew of the devious nature of Karl O'Brian, which now extended to Hopkins. Their unholy alliance would force them to protect each other and this made them dangerous. But one question immediately tumbled from her lips. 'What could possibly be in this for Hopkins?' she asked.

'I have given this some thought,' said Alex, 'and can only conclude that it is personal gain.'

'No doubt. But what gain exactly? And how?'

Alex shifted uneasily in his chair. 'Mr O'Brian has been to the bank on several occasions since securing half ownership and total management over the Double U. He is now the certified account holder.'

Rita could see that Alex was anxious and becoming a little unsettled. 'Is that suspicious?' she asked gently.

'No, it shouldn't be, but on each visit, Mr O'Brian only deals with the manager in his upstairs office. The meetings are often long.'

'Do you know what is being discussed?'

Alex hung his head. 'No.'

'But you suspect, don't you, Alex?'

Alex nodded. 'I have heard some raised voices. I think they were demands.'

'From O'Brian?'

'No, I think Hopkins was threating O'Brian. In fact, I have concluded that our manager is blackmailing Mr O'Brian.'

'Go on,' encouraged Rita.

'It would seem that only three people knew of the document that is in the safety deposit box. Mr Youcheck, who drew it up; Mr O'Brian, who signed it, and received $1,000 in return; and Mr Hopkins, our manager, who registered the document when Mr Youcheck brought it to the bank for safe keeping.'

Rita nodded in support of the proposition.

'For Mr O'Brian to make claim over the Double U by saying there was a verbal agreement for co-ownership, which is a direct contradiction to the written agreement held by the bank, he needed Mr Hopkins' collusion.'

'Yes, I can't fault that deduction,' said Rita.

'I think Hopkins is now squeezing O'Brian for more money, a lot of money, but cattle sales have all but stopped from the Double U. I also think O'Brian wants access to the cash in the safety deposit box and our manager won't give it to him. On occasion O'Brian has come in smelling of liquor and left angry and cussing.'

Rita had to hide her smile at O'Brian being held to ransom by Hopkins.

'And frankly, I'm feeling a little fearful,' said Alex.

'How so?' asked Rita.

'The owner of the Double U and the Manager of the Grange Branch of the Missouri Savings and Loans are the two most powerful men in the valley,' said Alex.

'I know,' confirmed Rita.

'If they were to find out that I know about the agreement, I may be at physical risk from both of them.'

Rita leant across and put her hand softly on Alex's knee. 'I understand and maybe it's time for me to show the same courage as you, and make right a long-standing wrong after nearly twenty years.'

Alex didn't know what Rita was referring to and when he asked, she changed the subject by asking, 'Can Karl O'Brian get access to the deposit box?'

'Technically, yes, but I think Mr Hopkins is doing to Mr

O'Brian what he is also doing to Mrs Youcheck.'

'Which is?' asked Rita.

'Withholding access to a customer's account.'

Rita nodded. 'That would make sense. It gives Hopkins control.'

'And apart from any blackmail money received, I think he may want to get his hands on the railroad bonds and other equities.'

'Of course,' agreed Rita, 'I bet he does.'

11

DO SOMETHING

The Need For A Plan

When Rita had finished telling me what Alex had told her, well, what a fit of rage I felt flood over me. I was on my feet and stomping around in circles. I had trouble controlling my pique and wanted both justice and vengeance all at the same time. 'I will go to the bank and demand to see that document,' I announced.

'You will do no such thing,' said Rita with annoyance.

'Why not?' I fumed.

'Do I need to explain, again? You will place Alex, me, and yourself in great danger. And do you really think for a moment that Hopkins will let you near that document or those bonds and cash? For God's sake, Nettie, sit back down.' There was fire in Rita's eyes as she spoke. 'Hopkins will guard that piece of paper with his life. It cannot only make him wealthy but also ruin him. Knowledge of its existence is knowledge of his interference, perjury and collusion with Karl O'Brian. From here on in Hopkins has no choice but to lie, cheat, steal, and maybe even kill if necessary, to carry this secret to the grave.'

Slowly, I was starting to understand that we had uncovered a hornets' nest, but how do you deal with a nest of hornets when it is now tangled in your hair? 'I still don't get it, Rita. If it is so dangerous, why doesn't he just destroy it?'

'It gives him power over Karl O'Brian, and that gives him access to the fortunes of the Double U. It is a perilous piece of paper, but one that provides him with a path to wealth and power. And besides, possession is nine-tenths of the law. He is safe while he has it under lock and key and held tightly in his custody.'

Rita was right, and I despaired at the situation. 'Hopkins and his greed are one thing, but how could my father do this to me? He has been paid off by Clement for one thousand dollars and put his mark upon a written agreement to leave us alone. Why does he have to make my life such a misery?'

Rita just looked straight ahead and remained silent.

I continued howling my injustice. 'All my life he has treated me with scorn, but I have never understood why. And now this.' I could feel my anger growing. 'But Clement must have known the true character of my father all along.'

Rita still remained mute and stony faced.

I tried again to get a response. 'I said, my husband must have known what my father was like.'

Rita lifted her eyes to look at me as she said coldly, 'I heard you, and yes Clement was a good judge of character. Not everybody has that knack.'

'What do I do now, Rita?'

'Short of murder, I'm not sure. I just know that we have to get the Double U back to its rightful owner, you, Nettie Youcheck.'

'That's what led me to the bank to get a loan, so that I

87

had the capital to build this farm up and show that I can successfully manage a property.'

Rita returned her gaze to something unseen but far away. 'Well, at least one good thing has come out of all of this.'

'What?' I asked.

'We now know what we are up against and why.'

I just felt defeated. My head of steam had ebbed and I was no more than an empty kettle, while Rita was tapping a long finger against her cheek, deep in thought.

Dejected, I said to Rita, 'I even tried looking up bible stories to see what to do. How the weak could win over the powerful.'

Rita's finger was still vigorously tapping away. 'Did you find anything?'

'Just one tale.'

'What was that?'

'David and Goliath.'

Rita's tapping finger started to slow. 'David and Goliath?'

'But Hollis said I should dismiss such silly thoughts of slinging a rock into the eye of a giant and cutting off his head.'

'Have you been back to the Double U at all?' asked Rita.

'No, not since Hollis and me packed up and came over here.'

'You know that most of the old hands have left.'

I was surprised, and my voice showed it. 'No, I didn't, but Dutch is still there.' I looked at Rita. 'Isn't he?'

Rita shook her head. 'Nope. He left about a month ago. Said he couldn't work with Karl O'Brian anymore and that the Double U was being run into the ground. Dutch took the last of the men hired by Clement with him. They moved south to Bentley. There's work down there, of sorts, but not as good as on the Double U.'

'And he didn't even come and see me before he left.' I said in bewilderment.

'What could he say, your home is being run to rack and ruin? He wouldn't have wanted to worry you. And he knows better than to get involved in matters where kin are known to be at loggerheads. Don't blame Dutch.'

'Why didn't you tell me this before now, Rita, that Dutch and the boys had left?'

'Like Dutch, I was protecting you, but things have changed. In fact, we may be able to turn this to an advantage.'

'How exactly?'

'Karl is still scrambling around to find cowhands. The ones he's picking up I know well. They all come to my place. None of them are of the calibre of Dutch and his boys. They are mostly lazy, dishonest, malcontents who wouldn't work to breathe if they didn't have to.'

'So where is the advantage?' I asked.

'You can't run the Double U without good men. It will start to lose money and if Hopkins is blackmailing Karl then he too is going to have trouble getting his pay.' Rita looked at me and she had that fierce look back in her eyes. 'We need to drive a wedge between Karl O'Brian and Albert Hopkins. Just like David did when the Israelites were facing the Philistines in the Valley of Elah. We need to cause a rift between Hopkins and O'Brian, that's what we need to do.'

I sat there a little bewildered. Would a rift work in allowing the weak to win over the strong? A slingshot seemed far more practicable. Although I did like the Valley of Elah reference because I had grown up living in a valley. I also vividly remember thinking this has got real personal with Rita, but I didn't understand why.

Now, I do have to say at this point that I was not completely naive when it came to the ways of the world and in particular the flesh, even at that early stage of my adult life. The thought had crossed my mind that Rita and Clement may have had a tryst once upon a time, in the past, and that a flicker of that flame still glowed in Rita's bosom. And I bet you may have thought the same too, being what human nature is, and thinking about the things that grown up men and women get up to. So, did a possible past relationship cause me any resentment? The answer was a simple no. What was in the past remained in the past. What I did know was that when I got married I got a devoted husband, albeit for such a short space of time. While the intensity of our love could not be measured by years, it could be measured by the strength of unconditional love. Clement and Rita were old enough to be my parents technically, so something may have happened long ago when I was just a tyke. In all, I just concluded that Rita's affection for my husband had remained and now extended to me as his young wife. It was only later that I was to find out what was really driving her to become so ferociously involved in my affairs. However, I do think at that particular moment she was within a hare's breath of telling me, right there and then. But thankfully she didn't. It was another secret that would have been beyond my comprehension to receive and accept at that particular moment. So, I will get to that later.

'Just how do we drive this wedge between Albert Hopkins and my father?' I enquired.

Rita spoke slowly and deliberately. 'We must take every opportunity to disrupt the workings of the Double U so that it is no longer producing the wealth that flows to the bank.'

'How do we do that?' I asked.

'We find some way to disrupt the workers.'

'We could keep the cowhands drunk all the time?' I suggested with enthusiasm. 'Drunks are useless workers.'

'How?' Rita's face sort of screwed up a bit.

'By, well,' my thoughts were travelling by the seat of their pants. 'Giving them free liquor.'

'That sounds expensive,' came the rich voice of Hollis.

We both looked up as he walked into the room.

'Have you been listening?' asked Rita.

'Been trying not to, especially when I heard that David and Goliath were back on the scene.'

'Did you hear anything else?'

'Only enough to know that we are going to war,' responded Hollis to Rita's inquisition.

'How so?' I asked.

'If you are planning to split up two people who are in cahoots and doing you wrong, you are going to have to be forceful.'

We both nodded.

'The Double U is a rich property. Master Clement put a lot of hard work into building it up, and it will still make money even with a lazy crew on board who do no more than water and attend to the livestock. You is going to need more than lazy to cut off the money supply.'

'Do you have any suggestions on how to do that, Hollis?' asked a sceptical Rita.

'There is only one way I know to bring the Double U to a standstill quick, but I'm not sure if I should say.'

'Say,' said Rita.

I pitched in my support. 'Say, Hollis,' I chorused.

'Well, I've seen plantations fail in a season when the slaves were emancipated and walked off. The owners had no one to pick the cotton. They had no crop to take to market. And when you've got no crop to take to market you've got nothing to sell. And when you've got nothing to sell you don't get paid. And when you don't—'

'OK,' said Rita, 'I've got the gist, thank you Hollis,' Rita's finger began tapping on that cheek again. 'So how do we get the cowhands to walk off?'

'You scare them off, said Hollis.

'And how do we do that?'

'I don't know,' said Hollis. 'I'm just telling you what needs to be done, not how to do it. That's white folks' business.'

'Thanks,' said Rita, when she didn't mean thanks at all.

'What scares you, Hollis?' I asked.

'Everything.'

'Surely not.'

'Does.'

'Everything?' I questioned again.

'I get scared of getting hungry, getting cold, getting old. Right now, I'm getting scared of you two, scheming.'

'Why? We haven't done anything yet.' I said.

'Sure 'nough at the moment, but whatever you want to do, I can bet that you'll have poor old Hollis involved in it somehow.'

'Not yet,' I said.

'Although, we may need Hollis's help a little later,' said Rita.

'See,' said Hollis, 'I knew it.'

'But you've always helped, Hollis. You helped Clement, then Nettie, and even me,' said Rita.

Hollis shrugged. He was not convinced.

Rita looked concerned. 'Maybe we've just never shown you the appreciation you deserve.'

'All the appreciation I want, I get.'

'Which is what?' I asked.

'Food, warmth and somewhere safe to get old.'

92

'Safe,' said Rita. 'That's what we need to do, make the cowhands feel like they are not safe.'

'How do we do that?' I asked.

'Just like Hollis said, we scare them.'

'How?' I asked again.

'Make them feel unsafe.'

I could see that we were going around in circles. What I couldn't see was how you could make anyone feel unsafe unless you were shooting at them and said so.

'You're right,' said Rita. 'That's what we need to do.'

Hollis looked concerned. 'Don't look at me,' he said. 'I'm not shooting at anyone. Besides, I'd be shaking too much to shoot straight. What about you, Miss Rita?'

Rita shook her head. 'Not me. The only gun I can shoot is the derringer in my reticule.'

'That just leaves Miss Nettie. Now, she is a dead-eyed dick.'

I squinted my face and questioned slowly, 'And what is it that I'm supposed to do precisely?'

'Just like you said,' said Rita. 'You start shooting at the cowhands. Just a potshot or two to scare them away.'

'What if they don't scare easy and take a potshot back at me?'

'Then you fire back.'

'And what if they fire back again.'

'You fire back again.'

'Lot of firing back and forth,' I said. 'And that does sound a bit like a war to me.'

'No, not a war,' said Rita. 'We don't want to kill anyone. Giving a cowpoke a nick or two is OK, but no killing. And you only want to fire on one at a time, when nobody else is around.'

I needed a little clarity. 'Fire when nobody else is around and just nick them?'

'Yes,' said Rita confidently. 'I think that should work out fine and send them scurrying away. I mean, who would possibly want to work under such occurrences? Thinking that they may be shot dead when going about their business while on their own.'

'Might work,' said Hollis. 'If anyone can do some nicking, then it's Miss Nettie. She's a mighty fine shot.'

I felt like I was back in school and needed to raise my hand to get back into the conversation. 'And what if I happen to shoot one of these cowhands dead? Do I plead my innocence on the basis that I was just trying to scare him?'

'I'll grant you that it's not the best plan ever, Nettie,' said Rita. 'But at the moment we have no other, and we need to do something.'

I looked at Hollis. 'What do you think, Hollis?'

He shrugged. ' 'Tis risky, but Miss Rita is right. We sure enough need to do something or you is never going to get back to the Double U. Your daddy has it in for you, Miss Nettie, and I have no idea why. But he's never going to let you back. I know it in my bones.'

12

THE HENRY

The .44 Plan

There was no doubt about it, I had been railroaded into the job of a could-be-assassin, especially if I failed in my marksmanship to nick a cowhand and scare him off.

'You know what would be really handy?' I said to Rita and Hollis without trying to hide my sarcasm.

'What?' they said in chorus.

'A gun.'

'You've got a gun, haven't you, Nettie?' queried Rita.

'Had a gun,' I said. 'A .44 Henry that Clement gave me, but I don't have it anymore, it's over at the Double U.'

'You didn't bring it with you?'

'Wasn't a good time to ask what we could take,' said Hollis shaking his head, 'we were being kicked out.'

'Oh,' said Rita. 'Then we'll just have to go over there and get it, won't we, Hollis?'

'I was just waiting for that,' said Hollis. 'I could see it coming like a locomotive full of steam, and me standing on the tracks just waiting for it to happen.'

'Then it shouldn't have been a surprise.' Rita could be a little too direct at times.

'But it'll be locked in the gun cabinet and my father will have the key.'

Hollis went to speak, then stopped short and raised his eyes.

Rita noticed. 'Hollis?'

'I was doin' nothing,' he replied slowly.

'Hollis?' Rita was not going to let go.

Hollis relented. 'OK, I was thinking. I know where the spare key is kept, hidden on the back corner of the cabinet.'

I said, 'I didn't know that.'

'It's for emergency, just in case a rifle is needed unexpectedly and real quick, and when getting the key from the desk drawer could take time.'

'Good,' said Rita. 'It should be dead simple collecting your rifle.'

Hollis had a question. 'Just say we go over and creep in and find the key, and take the rifle, and—'

'And what?' asked Rita with a tinge of displeasure.

'Don't you think Mister Karl is going to notice it missing?'

I thought about it for a little and kind of agreed. 'Might.'

Hollis said, 'See.'

I replied, 'Might not, either. My father is not a noticing kind of a man.'

Hollis raised his eyes. In fact, he was doing a real lot of eye raising during this conversation.

'A lot of guns in that cabinet,' I added. 'Rifles, carbines, old muskets, shotguns, even some handguns. And if you didn't know what was in there to begin with, missing just one in particular may not be a problem. Even to a noticing kind of man.'

'Let me tell you about another problem,' said Hollis.

'What are we going to say if we get caught, red-handed, so to speak?'

'Oh, we can't afford for that to happen,' I said.

'Nettie is right, Hollis. You can't afford to get caught.'

Hollis was looking all questioning. 'When did the *we* change to just *me?*'

'I'll help,' I said. 'I can drive the buckboard and have it waiting, as soon as you come out of the homestead with my rifle, we—'

Hollis cut me short with a 'thanks,' but it really didn't sound much like an acknowledgement of my support.

I had never been on a raid before, but I had read my fill of Indian raiding parties against the early settlers and knew the rudimentary requirements. Ours would not be a hoot and hollering raid but one of quiet stealth and cunning. We would sneak in and sneak out, without leaving any sign that we had even left our beds. I say beds, because this would have to be done under the cover of darkness.

I knew that Rita was sharing my enthusiasm, but I was less sure of Hollis's fire for excitement. Anyway, I was up for it and ready to go that very night, only to have Hollis propose that it was best not to rush and that we should sleep on it. The next evening, I was again ready to go, but once again Hollis said he wanted to do a little more sleeping and contemplating.

I said, 'You are either sleeping or contemplating, but you can't be doing both, and judging from your red eyes you've been doing more contemplating than sleeping.'

'That's a fact,' he agreed.

'Are you getting cold feet?' I asked.

'I've had cold feet all my life and it has kept the rest of my body warm till now.'

'If we don't do it tonight, then it is on for tomorrow,' I decreed. 'Delaying will do no good. Besides, we still have some good moonlight left.'

'OK,' said Hollis finally. 'We will go over tonight, but this is what I propose. We do it just casual like, and take a look see. Get a feel for the lie of the land, then tomorrow, we do it straight up.'

It all sounded silly to me, but Hollis was older, and I guess wiser, so I said yes, reluctantly.

The time selected to leave on our incursion was midnight as that seemed to be a suitable hour. However, by ten we were both feeling tired and decided to get the campaign under way. This turned out to be fortuitous as the timings I had in my head were all out by a long way. It seems that raiding, especially at night, takes a lot longer than just going and doing something during the day.

The moon was in the third quarter and with the cloudless night it made for good seeing. So much so that I blackened my face with soot from the coal bucket so that I would blend into the shadows. I hadn't told Hollis of my intention to use make-up and near scared the socks off him when I got up on the buckboard.

'Lordy, Lord. You look like a ghost,' he said dramatically, clutching at his chest. 'You realize you could have put me in an early grave?'

'Why?' I said. 'I can't be a ghost, ghosts are white.'

'Your ghosts are white,' he said. 'Not mine.'

We started out on the road to town before turning off at the fork to take the back track to the Double U. Just near the old well we went cross-country for a short way until we were on the high ground just before the bottom creek, where we stopped. The homestead was silhouetted before us.

'I'll come with you,' I said.

'Why?' asked Hollis.

'I just want a look see,' I said.

'No, just let me go. You go back and look after Daisy and the buckboard.'

'Daisy is fine, and I want to come with you.' Really, I just wanted to see my home again. It was like a magnet drawing me towards it and there was nothing I could do to stop it. 'I just want to take a look.' Then said softly, 'please?'

'Come on then and don't make any noise. And if we get separated for any reason, you go straight back to the buckboard and go home.'

'What about you?'

'Don't you worry about me, I'll find my own way back if I have to.'

We walked down the rise, crossed the creek on the stepping stones and approached that familiar place. All was in darkness and all was quiet.

'OK, we've seen it close up,' said Hollis, 'we can go now.'

'It looks lifeless,' I said. 'I've never seen it like that, but I guess that's what it is like in the middle of the night.'

'Come on, let's go,' urged Hollis.

'Why? To come back again tomorrow night?' It just didn't make sense.

'That was the plan,' said Hollis.

'But we are here now. We just need to go and do it.'

'Right now?'

'Yes, then it is over and done with.'

I could see Hollis's face in the moonlight and he was pondering. 'Suppose,' he finally relented, 'because you and Miss Rita are not going to change your minds on this, are you?'

'Nope,' I said.

'Not ever?'

'Nope, not ever.'

Hollis let out a long sigh and straightened himself fully upright.

'I'll come with you,' I said.

'No, stay here, it's safer.'

'It'll be safe if I come with you. Just a little way that's all.'

I followed Hollis across to the corner fence, along to the side gate that was open. It should have been closed to keep the skunks and raccoons out.

Hollis stopped, but I continued to walk over to the front garden beds. Hollis followed and said, a little agitated, 'What are you doing?'

Looking down on the barren plot, I said quietly, 'All my flowers have died, Hollis, and all they needed was just a little regular water.' Without thinking I stepped up onto the veranda and crossed to the front door.

'Miss Nettie,' called Hollis in a whisper and I knew that he was calling me back, but it was no use, I felt compelled to enter. It was like coming home after being away for a long time. I turned the handle and the door opened with a soft creak and I stepped inside.

I crept slowly through the vestibule, past the coat pegs where Clement used to hang his holster and gun and into the front room. Standing there in the dark, waiting for my eyes to adjust, I felt Hollis join me. We both stood, and I found his hand hanging by his side and gripped it. He squeezed it back.

'Our home,' I said softly.

'Yes, it is,' he replied in a deep whisper.

As my eyes became accustomed to the shadowy light, which was helped by the moon glow through the windows, I could see the familiar shape of the furniture and also the disarray. Books lay scattered from the shelves along with plates, a vase and bottles. Lots of whiskey bottles that littered the floor. What a mess, I thought.

Hollis edged his way across the large room to the gun cabinet on the far wall while I followed. He ran his hand down the corner edge close to the wall, found the secret key and removed it from its little hook.

We both took up a position in front of the tall cabinet and peered for the keyhole. It was nowhere to be seen. I eventually found it by running my finger up the edge of the door, but only after a couple of goes. When Hollis inserted the key and turned the lock, it seemed to make an almighty metallic click. He pulled back on the door and dislodged a book that was sitting on the narrow shelf that we hadn't seen. It fell to the floor with a clunk and we froze in fright.

I was sure that the game was now up and waited to hear my father come storming in to accost us. I held my breath in anticipation, and it was only after I thought I would bust that I realized we had not been sprung.

'Quick,' whispered Hollis. 'Get your gun and let's get out of here.'

I looked into the cabinet, but I couldn't distinguish which one was mine amongst the myriad of other weapons. 'I can't see it,' I said quietly.

'Well, take any one,' said Hollis.

'No,' I said, 'it has to be my Henry.' I began feeling each weapon in the hope of finding the right one but finally gave up and said, 'I will have to take each one out, take it to the window and have a look in the moonlight.'

'We can't do that, we don't have the time.'

'Yes, we do, it won't take long.'

But it did. Why is it that no matter what you are looking for, when searching a pile of like items, that it is always the last, or at least next to last, to be found?

'Got it,' I finally declared.

'Thank the Lord,' mumbled Hollis. 'Now we can go.'

'No, I need ammunition.'

Hollis sighed long and low.

Finding the ammunition wasn't as difficult as finding my Henry, and I loaded up my pockets, and those of Hollis. The cardboard boxes of bullets were heavy and made us waddle when we walked.

Just as Hollis was closing the cabinet door, I saw the outline of a pistol resting on the bottom rack. I reached in and picked it up. The familiar feel told me immediately that it was Clement's Colt. 'I'm taking this, too,' I said.

'Why?' asked Clement.

'Because it belonged to my husband.'

Hollis just nodded, closed the door, turned the lock and returned the key to its secret place.

As we were leaving, I took a detour across to the hall that led to my bedroom and stood for a moment. It was as if I could feel Clement's presence and for a moment I wondered if he would appear, but he didn't. Instead, I just heard the familiar snoring of my father. I knew that sound so well. I had listened to it for years. It was the sound of an opened-mouth inebriate in a self-induced coma.

When I returned to find Hollis in the doorway of the front room, I told him not to worry, my father would not wake if the two of us decided to stay and throw a party. He had not changed his ways, I thought. He was a miserable man of whom the bottle had taken command over his weak will, and from the look of my once beautiful front room, he was exhausting the treasure of the Double U on liquor.

By the time we pulled the buckboard into our yard it was close to first light. I unharnessed our faithful Daisy, let her loose behind the barn and stashed our loot under my bed for safekeeping. Hollis stoked up the stove for me and by the time I got to the kitchen, the plate was hot enough to boil eggs for breakfast.

It was only later when I went to wash up that I got to see my blackened face in the mirror. I paused and looked closely and wondered what it must be like for Hollis, being black. To this day I have no real appreciation of what that might be, other than I have heard the hurtful, and sometimes hateful, things that people say. At that moment I felt as one with his kin and said a prayer that I may never forget this moment, this feeling. Being black, white or brindle should make no difference, it is only skin deep. My father could never be half the man of Hollis, it was just not in him. I don't know if he had been born with an inferior character, but I do know that he had certainly honed it to a fine edge over the ensuing years. Had I been fortunate enough to have a father of the calibre of Hollis, I would have been proud, and somehow, I believed he would have been proud of me.

13

SAGE HENS

My Smart Mouth

When I started telling you my story, it was at the time when I was shooting at my father's cowhands, or at least one in particular, a Texan. And now I've been able to explain the reasons why, and of the grand plan to chase away the hired help. However, I'm sure you are hankering to know if such a spurious plan was successful?

The actual implementation of this shady, sneaky, little scheme, which transgressed a number of moral boundaries, certainly disrupted productive work at the Double U, but did it hasten the demise of my father? In hindsight, it would have happened without a shot being fired. Karl O'Brian couldn't run his own life, let alone that of others who worked on that large property. Most of the workers would have left eventually, fed up with the disorganization and poor instructions. I am also sure many others, further afield, saw the shortcomings of Karl O'Brian and were becoming concerned and annoyed, like Albert Hopkins of the Missouri Savings and Loans Bank, and Zac Wilson, who replaced Dutch Bonner as the chief cowhand. However, each of these men saw my father's glaring faults in a different light. Hopkins was concerned that he would not be fully paid for the deal he had brokered with my father to hide an incriminating document and give false testimony in court. While Zac Wilson saw an opportunity to have an easy time working for a man who was a fool and drunk most of the time.

I didn't start shooting anybody first up. The winging came later. Initially, I just shot at objects such as a water canteen or a coffee pot. After that I graduated to things that were closer at hand. When a man has a tin mug of hot coffee shot from his grip, he is liable to jump in the air and duck for cover. I also put a shot or two over their heads – close mind – sometimes so close to the ear that they could feel the rush of wind from the bullet as it cracked the air.

When word of this shooting harassment started to filter back to those in Grange, the town sheriff, Owen Reed, rode to the Double U see my father. Owen listened quietly to the demands being made for him to apprehend the culprit, before speaking to two of the cowhands who had been shot at, but they were unable to provide any insight into why or who would do such a thing.

This difficulty was compounded by the lack of any sign from where the shots had been fired or any tracks of escape. On this aspect Hollis and I were scrupulous. We never took the buckboard across the boundary and onto Double U property but alighted and walked into an area that offered good cover and waited in ambush. Some days we saw nothing, on others a cowhand would wander into our trap.

Sheriff Reed said he had nothing to go on and suggested that each cowhand be more vigilant and that Zac, as the chief cowhand, should do a little local investigating.

This he did, visiting me and Hollis after another one of the hands had a round pass through the collar of his shirt and crease his neck. That shot gave me a bit of a fright as I had aimed to just put the bullet past his earlobe. I watched as he clutched his neck and was amazed at the amount of blood that quickly covered his shirt before he mounted with haste and departed at a gallop back to the safety of the homestead.

Zac was one of those over-confident men who saw himself as God's gift. He was cocky and handsome, in a pretty boy sort of way with his golden locks. I much preferred darker, rugged men. He didn't lift his hat when we first met. Instead he just pushed his Stetson to the back of his head, to show off his curls. 'Zac Wilson,' he said. 'I'm now the leading hand over at the Double U.'

'Oh,' I said. 'That must be nice for you.'

He smiled and shook his head slightly. 'You're my boss's daughter.'

I said nothing.

'Aren't you?'

'Forgive me, Mr Wilson, I didn't know you were asking,' I said. 'I thought you were making a statement of fact.'

Hollis was close by and I didn't have to look at him to know what he'd be saying all over his face. He didn't like it when I got all smart-mouthed with men, or anyone else for that matter. He said it was going to get me into a lot of trouble someday.

'Have you been experiencing anyone taking potshots on your property?' he asked.

'At what in particular?' I asked back.

'You or your boy, here.'

He was referring to Hollis, who was older and wiser than both of us combined.

'Now why would anyone want to take a potshot at a

young widow or an old man?' I said with a hint of sarcastic sanctimony.

'I have no idea. But I don't know why they are shooting at my men either. Nearly killed one. He could have bled to death.'

'Maybe it was a stray shot from someone hunting a sage hen,' I said.

He pushed his hat back a little further. 'I didn't know you still got sage hens in the valley any more. I thought they were all shot out.'

'Oh dear, were they? Maybe it's their kin from up in the hills fighting back.'

Wilson couldn't contain his smile. 'Well, if you see anyone suspicious, I'd be obliged if you could let me know.'

'Maybe I'll keep my eye out for the hens, too,' I said.

Still smiling, he turned to go, then stopped. 'Do you own a rifle?'

I felt my blood run cold. I'd been too slick by half.

'We have a shotgun,' said Hollis.

Zac Wilson kept his eyes on me. 'Maybe a .44?'

I tried to take a breath without gasping for air to fill my lungs. I counted to five slowly before I answered. 'Do I look like the kind of girl who could shoot a rifle, let alone own one?'

He thought about it for a moment or two then said slowly, 'No, probably not.'

When he rode off I did let out a puff from holding my breath.

'What the. . . .' said Hollis with a look of alarm all over his face. 'And all that sage hen stuff. You could have given us away.'

I knew that I had been too clever for my own good. 'It was just banter,' I said unconvincingly.

'He's suspicious.'

'That's only because he knows nothing, so he's suspicious of everything.'

'This is no time for messing around,' said Hollis. 'We need to be real, real careful. Maybe we should put a hold on the shooting.'

I didn't say anything, but I agreed. Zac Wilson was turning over rocks just to see what lay under them and I was under one of those rocks.

It was not until sometime later, maybe a week or two, that I became aware that when Zac was looking under our rock, he had taken a fancy to me. So much so, that he saw my father and said that he'd like his permission to call on me.

My father, who was drunk at the time, completely misread the request and his intentions, thinking that I had made the advances. This he saw as mischief with his leading hand, but he didn't raise any concerns with Wilson. A day or two later, when I was in Grange to sell off a box of corn ears to the general store for some much-needed cash, I was accosted by my father. He'd been saloon crawling as usual, and was told by a fellow traveller that I was in town. He came looking and by the time he found me, he had built up a fine head of steam.

He caught me just as I was about to leave the store and was making my way past a dozen or so customers. 'You keep yourself to yourself,' he bellowed.

His arrival and his manner caught me by complete surprise and I was totally confused as to what he meant. I went to speak but took fright when I saw the anger in his eyes.

'You are no different than your mother with your pretty words and a willingness to lift your skirt.'

I heard the women in the shop gasp as one, and I was mortified with the inference of his abhorrent remark. I felt myself shrink and wither. Me, an independent, widowed woman, confident of my abilities, yet somehow, I could not escape my past of being a young apprehensive girl who was submissive to her father's will. I felt my face flush red with embarrassment and my head and eyes drop in deferential obedience. I wanted to explain, but all my words had been snuffed out.

'You stay where you belong, tending to my farm and feeding the hogs; and stay away from my leading hand. Do you hear me?'

I nodded.

'Did you hear me?' he bellowed again.

'Yes,' I cheeped like a little bird.

He stormed off and I stood there cemented to the spot until Hollis came and got me. He had heard the whole thing from the back of the buckboard.

I was in such a state that I couldn't catch my breath between my uncontrollable sobs. 'Take me home,' I choked while clenching at Hollis's arm in case I should stumble and fall to the ground in my state of distress.

14

IRISH WHISKEY

For Occasions of Distress

What I really wanted to do was go home and curl up into a tight ball on my little cot and die. I had been accused of infidelity in public and humiliated in front of strangers. The gossip from this event would spread like wildfire, consuming Grange by nightfall and raging halfway up the valley by sunrise. My passage to womanhood as a wife to Clement and first lady of the Double U had been undone in one brief and malicious exchange with my father. The encounter had lasted no more than a minute, yet it had stolen back that precious experience of matrimony and independence, to return me to the reticent young girl I had been.

'Take me home, please,' I had sobbed to Hollis outside the general store, but he knew better.

'No,' he said. 'You need some mothering right now and I know the one person who can give that to you.'

Hollis turned the buckboard down towards the creek and cracked the reins. He pulled up at that same spot where he had first taken me to meet Rita. Then it had been

110

in a fine lacquered buggy, but now I sat in tears on an old bleached and creaking buckboard.

Hollis went in and Rita came out in a rush and helped me down. As soon as my feet touched the ground I felt her arms around me and I responded by gripping her in a deep hug. 'Oh, Rita, oh Rita,' I cried.

'I know, I know, I know,' said Rita as she patted my back. 'Hollis told me what happened.'

'How could my father talk to me like that? What have I done to him to deserve such a public scolding?'

'Shush, child, shush,' she said. 'Come inside.'

When we got into her small office she sat me on the little couch against the wall and went to the cupboard behind her desk. She pulled out one bottle, put it back, looked around, then selected another from the top shelf. With two small but heavy crystal glasses in her hand she joined me, poured from the bottle a dark liquid and offered me one with the words, 'This is my best bottle of Irish, I keep it for occasions of distress.'

'What is Irish?' I asked as I put the thistle-shaped glass to my nose and smelt. It reminded me of smoky oranges, not that I can say I had ever smelt a lot of smoky oranges in my life.

'Whiskey, now drink up, you need it.'

'Is it medicinal?' I asked innocently.

'Very much so,' said Rita. 'Now, down in one hit, on the count of three. Follow me. One, two, three.' With the glass to her lips, Rita tilted her head back and swallowed it all.

I followed suit. The sharpness of the alcohol was subdued by the creamy texture of honey and what tasted like melted butter. As I swallowed, I felt a warmth travel down the length of my throat. It was to be the first time that I tasted whiskey, but not the last. I went to speak.

'Say nothing, we need to do it again.'

We did, and I should have realized that if Rita was going to match me shot for shot, she too was in some sort of distress and in need of medicinal care.

By the third shot I had regained my composure and the sobbing had stopped. 'Why does my father hate me so?' I asked in a now contemplative way. 'Because to do what he did, drunk or not, was a thing of hatred.'

Rita remained tight-lipped.

'I just don't understand, Rita.'

Rita's face was frozen.

'I tried to be a good daughter. I worked hard, I did what I was told, I—'

Rita cut me off. 'Enough.'

The alcohol was taking effect and I was beginning to loosen up a little. 'I didn't do enough?' I questioned.

'You did more than enough. You did too much.'

I felt my brow furrowed.

'Enough self-scolding. You are Nettie Youcheck.'

'In name only,' I said. 'I feel like little Nettie O'Brian again.'

'No, you're not. You are Nettie Youcheck.'

'Easy to say,' I said waving my little glass around in the air.

'You listen up,' said Rita with a touch of venom that under any other circumstance would have startled me. 'You were never Nettie O'Brian. Never, ever.'

'Ha,' I mocked, feeling rosy as I held my glass out for a refill. 'Oh, how I wish that were true. But that's all I've ever been and will be until the day I die.'

With that Rita leaped to her feet, her empty shot glass dropping from her hand to thump upon the rug. She lunged forward and grabbed my face in both hands and squeezed my cheeks firmly with her fingers, saying as she looked me square in the eyes, 'You were never, ever, Nettie

O'Brian, do you hear me? Never. Ever.'

My cheeks were being squeezed hard to the point of discomfort. 'Then who am I?'

Rita's face loomed large in my vision and she kissed me full on the lips, and her tears began to tumble. 'Nettie, Nettie, Nettie. I love you as I loved your mother. I am your godmother by default and I have failed in my duties, but no more. Karl O'Brian is nothing to you. You are of far better stock. You are the child of another man.'

Suddenly, I felt a little woozy. Was I hearing right or was it the intoxication of the Irish whiskey? 'Rita, are you messing?' is all I could say.

Her lips were pressed tight as she shook her head.

'Who is my father?' I asked. 'Do you know?'

Rita nodded her head vigorously.

'Then please tell me.'

Rita slowly let go of my tender cheeks and plonked back down on the couch close to me. 'I had promised that I would never tell, but circumstances have changed.'

I was feeling a little giddy but quite relaxed.

'Your mother and I were close, very close, when we were young. We arrived in Grange around the same time in '68 and we were the same age, just nineteen. When she met Karl, I knew it was a bad match. But she could see no wrong in him, even when he was treating her mean, and he began doing that right from the start. Some people are just born nasty, and Karl O'Brian is one of them.'

'So why did they get married?' I asked.

'You mother was willing to excuse his bad manners, his bad moods, and his brutal ways. He was also a hard drinker back then, but he couldn't hold his liquor and it made him more cruel than normal. Nettie, your mother was pretty, very pretty, a grand prize, and Karl wanted that prize for himself. He sweet-talked her and promised to change his ways and she believed him. The day they got married, he got drunk as a skunk and that's what he became, forever – a skunk.'

Rita was not holding back. She was giving the man who I thought was my father both barrels.

'Your mother eventually came to her senses and confided in me that he was a drunken beast and that she lived in fear. I told her to leave him, but she wouldn't at first. She stayed loyal. However, by the second year of marriage she had become so frightened that I urged her to go, which is all well and good for me to say. However, where could she go?' Rita reached down and picked up her whiskey glass and filled it to the brim. I thought she was going to hand it to me and went to motion no, maybe no more, but this drink wasn't for me. Rita knocked it back in one gulp. 'Later,' she said with a wistful look on her face, 'a white knight arrived in the form of Mitchell Shaw. He was handsome, well-mannered and softly spoken. Your mother met him by chance at the general store and they instantly fell in love. It was a match made in heaven. But it was too late.'

I leant in to hear more while still clutching my empty glass.

'Mitchell came to me, knowing I was Nettie's close friend, and asked what he should do. I told him that he had stolen her heart and now he must steal her away from that skunk O'Brian.'

'What happened next?' I asked.

'He took her and I rejoiced, but my celebrations were short-lived. Karl flew into a furious rage and went after them, finally tracking them down in Springfield.'

'And?' I asked wide-eyed.

Rita looked around. 'Where's that bottle?'

'Do you think you've had enough?' I queried.

'Not nearly,' said Rita. 'And you could do well to join me

when you hear what I have to say.'

Could it get any worse I wondered, but decided to take Rita's advice and joined her.

'When Karl found them, he held back and waited until Nettie was alone and then confronted her. She nearly died of fright from being found. He seized her and took her to the sheriff and told him that they were wed. The sheriff questioned Nettie, who confirmed that they were married, but that she had run off for her own safety. The sheriff said she had to go back with her lawful husband to Grange and sort it out there.'

I sipped the whiskey and could feel the pain of my young mother being lassoed, hauled in and tied down.

Rita continued, 'When Mitchell arrived home at the end of the day, his neighbours told him what had happened. He went and saw the sheriff, who confirmed that Nettie had been taken back to Grange by her husband.'

'Did he go after her?' I probed as my heart raced.

'He did, and he caught up with them just out of Grange.'

'Was there an argument? A fight?'

Rita bit at her bottom lip in silence.

'Well was there, Rita?'

'No. There was no argument. No fight.'

'What happened?'

Rita went silent again.

'Rita, tell me.'

Rita looked away, paused, then looked back, and in a cold voice said, 'Karl O'Brian shot Mitchell Shaw dead.'

I gasped.

'Mitchell was unarmed, and Karl shot him in the face as he rode up to make his plea for Nettie, and he did it right in front of your mother.'

'When did you find this out?' I asked.

115

'Just after you were born and things started to go wrong. We couldn't stop the bleeding. At first, she just wanted me to look after you until she got back on her feet. When it became clear that she was very, very sick and wouldn't recover, she confided in me that her new baby girl was Mitchell's. She told me how Karl had killed an innocent, unarmed man in cold, malicious blood.'

'Did my father know I was not his daughter?'

'Not at first, but in time he did. You may have your mother's looks, but you have your real father's bright and agreeable nature.'

'Does he know that you know, Rita?'

Rita's head jerked. 'No. And he certainly doesn't know that Nettie told me of him murdering Mitchell Shaw.'

'Oh, Rita, this is such a terrible mess, what do we do?'

Rita's face seemed to be set like a rock and her gaze was as icy as a bitter winter wind. She turned to me and said with cold steel in her voice, 'Kill him.'

15

THE REAL
MESSAGE

Be Careful, Nettie

I awoke the next morning as if from a bad dream with a voice shouting inside my head, 'Kill him, kill him, kill him.' I went to sit up, but each time I tried it was as if a spike had been driven down through the top of my skull. What was going on?

'Are you going to get up now?' asked Hollis in a superior tone.

I tried to focus on the silhouette in the doorframe, but the light beyond hurt my eyes.

'It is past midday,' came the announcement in that deep voice.

It couldn't be. I looked down and saw that I was still fully dressed. I even had my boots on. I'd never gone to bed with my boots on before. 'What happened?'

'You got drunk.'

'I did?'

'And Miss Rita was well on the way, too, by the time I

finally got you up on to the buckboard.'

'I feel in no fit state,' I said.

'You were in fine form on the way home last night.'

'I was?'

'You sang to me, all the way.'

'I'm no singer.'

'Amen to that.'

My head was hurting, and I needed a little sympathy. 'Hollis, I feel terrible.'

'Look the same, too.'

He wasn't helping, being all virtuous and temperate. It was not appreciated. Time to turn the table. 'Are you telling me that you've never been like this?'

'When I was younger, but I grew out of it. Besides, it's just too darn expensive, unless you want to drink puddle juice from a jar.'

I didn't know what puddle juice was, but I could imagine. In fact, I think I could taste it in my mouth. 'What was I drinking, again?'

'I saw the bottle. Pricey, ten-year-old, Irish whiskey.'

'I remember now and I also remember other things. Hollis—'

'Yes?'

'Rita told me something most alarming last night.'

'Oh,' said Hollis, 'and what was that?'

'I don't know if I should say.'

'Then don't. If you have a doubt, keep it to yourself.'

Hollis was full of old, rhyming, homespun philosophies that had a ring of truth to them, so I decided to take his advice.

The next day I was still in a fragile state, finding it better to stay away from all types of food and take nothing more than weak tea or cool water from the well. Even the smell of coffee was hard to bear and any lifting work, where I had to bend over, caused my head to spin. I shuffled around in the vegetable patch with a hoe, and each time Hollis passed I tried to look diligent, but I was fooling no one except myself.

I didn't hear Dutch Bonner ride up or even hear Hollis call out to greet him. When he walked around the side of the homestead, I was fussing with a little water furrow that I had scraped out with slow and meticulous care.

Hollis mumbled under his breath to Dutch. 'Lips that touch liquor will never touch mine.'

'I heard that,' I said and looked up. 'Dutch!' It was certainly a surprise. 'What are you doing here? I thought you were down in Bentley.' I was trying to be as cheery as a schoolgirl.

'Am, but I needed to see you on the quiet.'

It was the way he said it that made me ask, 'Should I be concerned?'

'You tell me.'

'About what?'

'I had a call from Sheriff Owen Reed two days ago when he was in Bentley on law business. He told me that someone was taking potshots at the hired hands of Double U. Seems it started not long after me and boys left.'

'And?' I said trying to look as if cotton candy wouldn't melt in my mouth.

'Zac Wilson collected a .44 slug that was left rattling around the bottom of a coffee pot with a neat hole in it. He gave it to Sheriff Reed.'

I didn't say anything, and Hollis was also silent.

'Owen asked me if I knew of anybody who had a .44 rifle who could shoot the whiskers off a flea.'

I looked straight at Dutch. 'And what did you say?' Then sucked in a deep breath.

'I said, no, never seen any fancy shooting in my time at the Double U.'

I held that breath for as long as I could until it finally blew out from my bottom lip; the wind lifted a curl on my forehead to signal my guilt.

'But I lied, didn't I?'

I sucked the same breath back in, which just made matters look worse.

'There are few people I know that can target shoot as good as you, Nettie.'

I had to say something instead of just looking silly. 'And you think I'm using cowhands for target practice?'

'If it would help you get back the Double U, yes I do. And—' Dutch glanced down at his boots, 'I wouldn't blame you.'

'But you want I should stop?'

'I didn't say that. There's something going on here that I don't understand. I'm here because I feel obliged to pass on a warning.'

'What would that warning be, if by chance, it was me doing the shooting?' He knew it was me, and the only reason I was trying to act innocent was because my mind was still as foggy as hell from being on the wrong side of sobriety. I was not cut out for this drinking and lying game.

Dutch looked straight at me. 'A new man has just been signed onto the payroll over at the Double U, he could be unpredictable.'

'You mean, Wilson?' I scoffed.

'No, word has it that Wilson has left. Seems he had a difference of opinion with your father.'

This news caught me by surprise. 'So who is the unpredictable hand?'

'He's not a cowhand. He's a young would-be gunslinger who said he will hunt down the assassin for two hundred dollars.'

'Assassin?' I questioned. 'No one has been assassinated, yet.'

'No, but shooting someone in the neck is pretty close.'

'It was just a crease. He unexpectedly moved real quick,' I quipped, then bit my tongue.

'Your father has accepted his price and this gunslinger is from Texas where they shoot first and ask questions later.'

'Does he have a name?' I enquired.

'Tex,' said Dutch.

'That figures,' I half mumbled to myself.

'I gotta go,' said Dutch. 'I want to be back in Bentley by tonight.' He waved his hat above his head and turned to leave.

'Dutch,' I called, and he stopped and half turned back. 'Thank you.'

'I'm only passing on what a lot of others know. Word travels fast around here, even down to Bentley. So, you be careful, Nettie.'

'I don't know if I have a choice any more if I am ever to get the Double U back,' I said, and all of a sudden my head felt clear.

'No,' said Dutch, 'you properly don't.'

As he turned I called again. 'If I do get the Double U back will you come back to work it with me?'

'Isn't that the real reason I came? The real message I wanted to pass to you?'

I had been a little slow on the uptake, but I now got it. As I gave him a farewell wave I shouted, 'Then I'll be seeing you soon.'

When Dutch had departed, Hollis said. 'So, you do have a plan to get the Double U back soon? I should have known. That's why you and Rita were celebrating.'

'No, we were getting drunk for other reasons.'

'Like what?'

'Rita put forward a persuasive argument that Karl O'Brian should be killed.'

Hollis's jaw dropped. 'Kill your own father?'

'Rita told me that he is not my father. I am the daughter of another man.'

'Who?'

'A man named Mitchell Shaw.'

'Where is he?'

'Dead.'

'How?' asked Hollis.

'Karl O'Brian shot him?'

'Oh, Lordy Lord, this is getting messy again. How did I ever get involved in white people's business in the first place?'

'It is messy, isn't it?' I agreed. 'Maybe that's what life is like.'

'Not my life, at least not up to now, kind of.'

'OK. There is only one thing for it,' I said sort of philosophical like.

'What's that, precisely?' Hollis looked uncomfortable.

'This whole mess needs to be cleaned up once and for all.'

'Amen to that, but who is doing the cleaning? *You* or *we?*'

'I can't do this on my own, Hollis. I need you more than ever.'

'I should have seen that coming.'

'I understand if you don't want to help. I expect nothing and will hold you to nothing. The Double U is my fight.' I was being more than a bit dramatic and was aware that my chin was sticking out into the breeze.

'It's not that simple,' said Hollis quietly.

'Yes, I know, messy never is,' I said, trying to sound mature.

'No. Your father thing is messy. The Double U thing is just not that simple.'

I didn't know what Hollis was getting at. 'How so?'

'The Double U is Master Clement, and it is Master Clement that you, me, Rita, Dutch and the cowhands all respected and loved. If we don't get the Double U back, we don't get him back into our lives. And if that happens then our lives are left hollow forever.'

What Hollis said was like turning a lamp bright that had been left in the window. Oh, he was such a smart man. He was right. The Double U was more than just a property, or land or cattle – it was the place where Clement's spirit resided. Each of us, in his or her own way, needed him to remain in our lives and Hollis had placed the light to guide us to him. Were we weak people to want this – to rely on a dead man? Or was this just part of a messy everyday world where we know, in our hearts, that no life is ever lived in solitary confinement.

16

ACCORDING TO PLAN

A Little More Irish

'We just need to do it one more time, Hollis, just one more,' I pleaded.

'And what precisely are you going to do? Kill him?'

'No, not him. I just want to scare the Texan off and get him out of the way, first.'

'He's a gunslinger, not a cowpoke. And then what? Your father will go and get another Texan, or a hired gun from some other place. I heard you can get good gunfighters out of Kansas City now. In fact, you can get anything you want out of Kansas City, now. Even Irish whiskey.'

I chose to ignore the virtuousness of the whiskey reference. 'He's not my father, remember, and if I get rid of this Tex character, I will have sent a clear message that I am bringing this to an end.'

'Remind me, what end is that, precisely?'

'Getting back the Double U.'

'How, exactly?' Hollis was looking down his nose at me,

being taller and all.

'Well, first I wing the Texan and scare him away with a small wound. Then I deal with Karl O'Brian.'

'How. With a bigger wound?'

'You are asking a lot of hows, Hollis.'

'You bet I am. We are now on the slippery slope of the wrong side of the law.'

'But not by much.'

'Will that be your defence in court, so that they don't hang us by much?'

'We haven't done any hanging offences.'

'Yet.'

'That's right.'

'But I get the impression that you and Rita have your hearts set on killing Karl O'Brian.'

'Rita has, I'm a little more undecided.'

'That's a comfort. So, what's your solution?'

'Don't know, yet.'

'I get the strong sense that we are travelling in the dark here without a lantern.'

'No, on the contrary, I can see the light,' I said in justification. 'That's why first things first.'

Hollis shook his head ever so slightly and left to get the buckboard out, but he did so with no zest in his step. We drove up towards the top paddock at a snail's pace.

'Do you want to stay with the buckboard?' I said. 'I can go on my own.'

'No,' he said abruptly.

'All right, let's get going and don't sulk.'

'I haven't sulked since I was a little bitty,' said Hollis.

'Or pout, either.'

'Pouting is different. You can do that when you're older and desiring to express a point.'

It was no use arguing. I knew Hollis was none too happy,

so best to just let him get it out of his system and let me get on with it. Our plan was as before. Leave the buckboard on our side of the fence, hike across to the nearest well and sit and wait. Or alternatively, to one of the other two wells that were within an hour's walk. All the cattle work was kept close to water at this time of the year.

We sat at the first well for an hour, before walking to the next well and waiting for another hour. I was ready to move on, but Hollis told me that I was getting impatient. 'You're not much good at fishing, are you?'

'Never really tried.'

'Well you're not. You have to sit and wait for the fish to come to you.'

'He's not a fish,' I said. 'He's a Texan, named Tex.'

'Same thing,' said Hollis.

'I don't think so,' I said.

We waited another hour and a half, but nothing.

'Let's go back to the first well,' I uttered.

And Hollis relented.

When we were just about there I'd had enough. I didn't even know if this Texan would be riding around out here or actually waiting in ambush for us. 'Let's just go home.'

Hollis silently nodded in agreement. We went down along the dry creek bed to take a short cut back to the buckboard and were just coming over the rise when we saw him. In fact, if it had not been for Hollis, I would have walked right out in the open as the sun was in my eyes and my bonnet was pulled low. We both froze before slowly, very slowly, sinking to our knees and on to our stomachs.

'Is that him, do you think?' I asked, as we looked at the tall lone figure.

'Are you kidding?' said Hollis. 'Of course it's him; he's practising his quick draw. That's what gunslingers from Texas do.' Hollis added, 'I guess.'

'Then you don't really know, do you?'

'Good enough bet, though, he's dressed in black.'

I agreed it was a good enough bet. I'd read that black was a popular colour for hired gunslingers, but for the life of me, I couldn't remember where I'd read it.

'We are awful exposed up here.' Hollis was getting anxious, but he had no need, we held the upper hand – surprise.

'We are just fine,' I said. 'No one knows we are here, least of all him. Just take a look. Have you ever seen anything more silly? Mister fancy pants, skiving around and drawing his handgun in and out of his holster.'

'Are you going to shoot him or not?

'I'm going to put a bullet in him all right.' I laid my cheek gently upon the stock and sighted on the target. I closed my left eye and took in a full breath just as Clement had taught me. I let the breath half out, paused, picked my mark on the outside of the upper right arm, the one he was using to draw his pistol, then focused on the foresight and gently squeezed the trigger.

The Henry kicked to the report as the cartridge fired and the .44 bullet shot straight and true towards its target one hundred and eighty yards away.

The gunslinger leapt in the air and gave out a yelp, dropping his gun and going to ground behind his saddle that was lying some five or six yards away.

I pulled down on the lever to reload. Hollis lent over and picked up the spent cartridge.

'Now, we need to get out of here, quick in case he comes after us,' said Hollis.

'Mister gunslinger over there is just like the others, he isn't going to come after us. He'll lie there till nightfall, before he makes a move to run back to the Double U.'

'Not if he's bleeding to death.'

'I just creased him, that's all.'

'What about the one you creased on the neck? He took off like a jackrabbit.'

'Necks are different to arms.'

'Are you a now doctor?'

I chose to ignore the remark, it contained sarcasm, which, as they say, is the lowest form of wit. We crawled away, with care, down to the creek, covering our tracks back to the buckboard.

'One down,' I said with a touch of pride.

'One down,' repeated Hollis in a flat voice.

Neither of us dared to discuss what we were going to do about Karl O'Brian, the man who had murdered my father and taken away from me what was rightly mine, the Double U. However, the Karl O'Brian final solution was to bog me down as if in a quagmire of molasses. With a little bit of ruminating, I could work myself up to the point of going over to the Double U homestead, walking in the front door and shooting that man without a by your leave. The trouble was, what then? Even if I wasn't caught straight up and charged with murder in the absence of some bona fide suspects, I was bound to be questioned at some point in time. I kept having dreams of Sheriff Reed shaking his head and saying, 'Now don't you go fibbing to me, Nettie or you will just make matters worse.'

To which I would say, 'There were reasons, Sheriff, I was provoked.'

'Tell it to the judge, Nettie.'

'Will he believe me, Sheriff Reed?' I could hear myself pleading.

'It's not him that you have to convince, it's the jury.'

The jury. I had seen juries in action and I preferred not to go there. In desperation I went and saw Rita.

Once in her office, she looked around and said, 'Do you want a drink, Nettie?'

'Definitely not,' I said.

'Probably right,' agreed Rita.

'We need to discuss the killing of Karl O'Brian,' I said. 'We need to work out how to do it.'

'Was it you who shot the Texan?' Rita asked.

I nodded.

'He's real angry and a little embarrassed. He was supposed to get the Double U gunman. Or in this case gunwoman. He's been in town saying it was one hell of a battle out there on the range and he gave as good as he got.'

'Well that's trash if ever I heard it. I winged him and he hid behind his saddle. Never fired a shot back. What cheek. Gee, those Texans sure know how to fib.'

'All men are liars,' said Rita. 'Sure you don't want a drink?'

I was fuming up and a little nip might help to settle me down. 'Only a small one,' I said.

'Only ever serve small,' said Rita.

I immediately thought that maybe fibbing was not exclusive to men.

When I put my lips to the glass it was in trepidation and I thought for a moment that I would have to pinch my nose. I closed my eyes and took a tentative sip. That familiar smooth warmth rolled down my throat. 'That wasn't too bad after all,' I said with amazement.

'You have to shoot that skunk O'Brian like you shot the Texan, but shoot him dead. That shouldn't be too hard.'

'That's not the hard bit,' I replied. 'That comes when Sheriff Reed comes a calling and asking questions.'

Rita nodded in agreement and took a sip. 'Alibi, Nettie, that's what you need.' Rita took another sip. 'You can say you were attending to your garden patch.'

'I thought of that,' I said. 'But who will believe me, I need to have a witness who will vouch for me.'

'Hollis?'

'Hollis says it won't work on account he is black and employed by me.'

'How much do you pay him?' asked Rita curiously.

'Nothing. He may as well be in servitude. But he won't go. He has fond memories of Clement.'

'He and Clement were boys together,' said Rita as she twisted a curl of her hair in reminiscence. 'Hollis was older and looked after Clement like a big brother. Dragged him from the creek when he was four, I've been told. He could of drowned there and then had it not been for Hollis.'

'I didn't know that,' and took a longer sip.

'True.' She continued twisting the strand of hair.

'I would have given up if it was not for Hollis,' I said. Then added, 'and you, Rita.'

Rita clinked her glass against mine in appreciation. 'Drink up, we need inspiration to figure out this conundrum.'

Well, I'm not going to go into all the detail of what occurred at that meeting, other than it is suffice to say that a plan evolved between sips of whiskey. However, this time I did pace myself a little better. Who actually thought of what, I doubt if either of us could remember accurately, but nonetheless we came up with a course of action. Did the whiskey have a bearing on our thoughts? Well, yes it did. And it would be fair to say that not all aspects of our intended actions were thought through to the very end, but this is how it worked out.

It was decided to write a letter to Karl O'Brian at the Double U, which I would slide under his front door. The aim of this letter was to confront him with the knowledge that his two most closely held secrets, of killing Mitchell Shaw and of the agreement to forfeit all rights to the Double U, were known to the mystery man who was taking potshots at his cowhands.

We both agreed that this would have a confronting effect and drive him further to the bottle, of which he needed little help, judging from the number of empties I saw the night Hollis and me got the Henry.

A second note would then be sent, saying that the mystery man was now coming after him personally as he had been a close friend of Mitchell Shaw and needed to right a twenty-year wrong. This second letter would put fear into Karl's heart. I would then fire a series of shots through the windows of the Double U homestead in the middle of the night while he was there, with the aim of frightening the bejesus out of him. This methodical and mounting pressure would force him to flee in order to save his life and leave the valley and never return. Or so we hoped.

I know in hindsight it all sounds somewhat fanciful, but a glass or three of Irish can make sense of the most difficult mysteries of the universe. And besides, it was the only plan we could come up with.

Anyway, now let me tell you exactly what happened, remembering that very few plans actually go accordingly.

17

A SORDID AFFAIR

Watch Your Footing

Rita had spoken briefly to Alex Milton when banking the weekend's earnings and asked him to drop by and see her that Monday evening. When he arrived she closed the door of her office and explained to him our plan of action. He immediately saw a complication to this whole story of a *mystery* gunman seeking revenge on Karl O'Brian for his past sins by asking, 'How would this gunman know about the agreement between Karl O'Brian and Clement Youcheck, and what if O'Brian tells Albert Hopkins of the written threats he has received under his door?'

'Suppose he does?' said Rita rather glibly, not seeing a problem.

'It will put me at risk, Rita,' said Alex gravely.

'How?' asked Rita.

'Knowledge of the agreement is a closely guarded secret. That's why Hopkins is holding it under lock and key in the bank vault. It would be natural to assume that any awareness of its existence could only come from a source that had access to the vault, and I am one of the few employees who goes in and out on a daily basis. In fact, you

132

could count the number of staff on one hand, and that includes the manager himself.'

'Oh,' said Rita, who quickly tried to recover ground by saying, 'but that's part of the *mystery*, which makes it all the more *mysterious*. Just how did the Double U gunman find out?'

This higgledy-piggledy explanation didn't cut it with Alex. His apprehension remained. However, somehow Rita still managed to receive his agreement to help where possible. Exactly how much of his blessing to this plan was related to a shot or two of Irish I don't know, but Rita did have her ways of persuasion, especially with men. I saw it up close over the years and while she didn't have to flutter her eyelashes, she could just sort of look and smile and move up close a little and say a few soft words directly into their ear, and pow, they were putty. It was amazing. Not that I'm saying she ever did anything devious. In fact, these poor souls seemed to love it. Sometimes, her powers of persuasion were a lot like that Irish whiskey – it had an intoxicating effect if you know what I mean – one that went well beyond the rationality of common sense.

Rita wrote the letter while Alex looked on. When finished, he said the handwriting looked too ladylike and suggested that he type the letter at the bank on their Remington typewriter, but that must have been the whiskey talking, because the following day he told Rita that he was just an amateur typist and if he was caught at the machine and the letter was taken to the manager, then the jig would be up. Alex had started to use colourful language and when I first heard him use words like 'jig', I could only conclude that he was reading too many of those illustrative detective magazines that had become popular with young men at that time. In the end, Alex rewrote the letter, but when it was handed to me and I read it, I'm darned if I could tell if the handwriting was masculine or feminine. It just looked like writing to me.

The letter was undated but signed with the initials TJ. This was done to drop the hint that it could stand for Trevor James. Rita said that Mr James had travelled with Mitchell Shaw when he had first come to Grange all those years ago. However, James moved on and had never been heard of again. Alex thought that it was a smart contrivance. I wasn't asked my view, but it sounded sort of shrewd, I guess.

I delivered the letter by putting it under the front door as planned. This I did with the assistance of Hollis late at night, well after midnight. I don't know what I expected would happen to show that the plan was working, but we needed some sort of reaction to see if our scheme had any chance of success.

A week later I delivered the second letter, with the intention that I would put a shot through the window and into the homestead the following night. However, the plan changed when Hollis caught up with Martha, who was still cooking over at the Double U. Martha told Hollis that Karl had been away for the week. When quizzed as to where, she didn't know.

The two letters were now waiting just inside the door and I wondered what would be made of this occurrence, when Karl O'Brian found them lying on the floor. Would it spook him, or would he dismiss the threats as foolish and from someone who couldn't even figure out if he was home or not? But all that changed when two days later Karl O'Brian turned up at the bank unannounced and agitated with a demand to see Albert Hopkins. Alex was able to report that their meeting had been brief and that when Karl had left, Hopkins had gone straight down to the vault on his own. Alex suggested that his purpose was to check on the security of the agreement document that he had used to blackmail Karl.

When I heard this, I raised concerns that Albert Hopkins might take this most important record from the bank vault and destroy it. But Rita convinced me that the document signed by Karl and Clement was far too important as it was his insurance policy. Without it, Hopkins held no sway over Karl.

Rita asked Alex, when he brought her the news of Karl's visit to the bank, 'Where is Karl now?'

'He crossed the street and went straight to the saloon,' said Alex with excitement, 'and he was still there when I went by on my way here.'

The next day was a Saturday, which is a busy day for Rita and her girls, so she got Alex to ride out and tell me of the news. He also passed a message from Rita that it was now up to me.

I thanked Alex and he asked whether I had a message to take back to Rita.

I didn't, but I had the feeling that I should say something. After all, she and Alex were in this as deep as I was, so off the top of my head, I said with determination in my voice, 'Tell her, it's now or never.'

Hollis, who was with me, said after Alex left, 'What does that mean? Now or never? Now or never, what?'

'It means, I guess, that I have to act as we had planned to do, tonight. I'll fire a shot through the window and frighten Karl O'Brian.'

'What?' said Hollis, 'frighten him to death? I'll bet that he'll be so drunk that you could shoot him dead and he wouldn't know. Remember when we got your Henry?'

Hollis was starting to pick holes in the plan, but regardless, I had to do something. So, after midnight we got out the buckboard, drove it over to the east well and walked over to the Double U homestead.

The window on the near side from where we approached would allow a shot to enter the main room and strike the wall near the gun cabinet.

Just as I was lining up, Hollis shook his head. 'No good. Better you put the shot through the bedroom window over his head if you want to give him a fright.'

He was right, it had to be a close, personal, sort of shot. We moved around the side to the bedroom window, and just as I was about to sight up again and fire, Hollis said, 'How do we know he is actually in his bed and not still in town?'

'I guess we just have to take the chance.'

'Can't do that,' said Hollis. 'We need to know for sure. This plan was shaky from the start and firing into an empty room isn't going to scare anyone. You've got to give the impression that the mystery gunman is seriously stalking his prey and knows what he's doing. Especially after delivering the mail while he was away.'

I could feel myself getting agitated. 'How are we going to find out for sure if he is in bed or not? Go down there, walk in through the front door and take a look?'

Hollis said nothing.

'Hollis. Did you hear me? Do you expect me to go in and take a look?'

Hollis still said nothing.

'Hollis?'

'I heard.'

'So why don't you answer my question?'

'Why? Because you've answered it yourself.'

All of a sudden, this whole scheme seemed as silly as trying to fetch water in a kitchen colander. 'We can't just go down there and go inside and see,' I said.

'We didn't get that Henry you're holding by sitting on this rise. Besides, have you got a better idea?'

I was being cornered and I didn't like it. Hollis had now got the courage that I lacked, or I thought he had, until he said, 'I'll stand watch for you.'

'Oh, no you won't, you're a-coming with me.'

'Only needs one to see,' said Hollis.

'Then you go and take a look and I'll stand guard.'

Hollis relented. 'OK, we'll both go, but I'll stay by the front room and make sure the escape route is secured. You can creep up to his door, like you did last time.'

I don't know why, but my nerves were a-jangling when I carefully stepped over the door sill that I had crossed so many times before. I should have been more composed. I had taken a bigger risk to get the Henry I now held in my right hand, but this time things just didn't seem right. The feeling of foreboding was suffocating, except I had no choice, so I sucked it up and pushed on. Hollis followed close behind.

Once into the front room we both stopped and stood dead still and waited for our eyes to adjust to the dark. Without the aid of the moonlight it was harder to see since our last visit, but I could still make out the familiar objects such as the couches, tables and chairs. As I edged forward in the still of the night, my foot struck an empty whiskey bottle that clinked sharply when it made contact with a second empty bottle.

Hollis let out a low, 'Shush.'

I continued forward, past the gun cabinet where I had taken the Henry rifle and towards the back passageway that led to the master bedroom. With each step my foot came in contact with scattered rubbish on the floor, most of which were empty bottles. Oh, how I would have loved to have taken a broom to the floor and given my home a good clean. It was a disgrace.

When I entered the passage, I prayed that I would hear

the sound of snoring. All I wanted to do was just confirm that Karl O'Brian was in the bedroom and asleep, but I could hear nothing. Maybe he was still in town, I told myself.

When I got to the door of the master bedroom, which was ajar, I paused again, peering into the dark and listening. However, there was just silence. I edged in a little more, pushing the door half open, and lent forward to gaze at the large bed. I took one more step, still straining to see.

It was empty.

'Darn,' I said under my breath and as I turned around to leave – that's when I saw Karl O'Brian. He was sitting in a chair against the wall and behind the open door, or should I say reclining with his head back, eyes closed and mouth open. A whiskey bottle stood upright between his legs and a rifle lay across his lap.

I let out a gasp of surprise and bolted. However, my shoulder clipped the edge of the door and sent it flying further open to strike the arm of the chair where Karl was perched on sentry waiting for the mystery gunman.

I heard the chair creak as he jolted upright and leapt to his feet, the bottle falling to the floor. He called out in a slur, 'I've got you now,' and I caught sight of the barrel of his gun as it came to his shoulder.

I was off like a jackrabbit, half in fright and half in determination to get away. I was back in the hallway when a shot rang out like a thunderbolt, to be instantly followed by the sound of shattered glass smashing to the floor. I had just entered the main room when I stepped on an empty whiskey bottle and felt my foot twist. I instantly lost my balance and could feel myself falling. I thrust out my free hand and tumbled to the floor with a thump.

'Nettie!' shouted Hollis from the centre of the room.

'Are you all right?'

I tried to get up but as soon as I put weight on my foot a streak of lightning ran up my leg and I fell to the floor again, this time dropping my rifle. 'Hollis, help,' I called back.

I heard the thumping of steps from behind me and knew I was done for. But in the dark and from my double fall I had become disorientated. I was actually facing back towards the passageway and the steps behind me were those of Hollis.

I felt his strong arms grab me and hoist me into the air. For a second, I thought it was Karl. Then I heard Hollis say, 'Let's go.'

I gripped at his shoulders for support and pulled myself upright and tried to hobble as best I could. We were nearly at the front door when I realized that I didn't have my rifle with me. It was on the floor where I fell. 'The Henry,' I anguished, just as a loud thump came from near the passageway and the sound of more breaking glass.

'No time,' said Hollis. 'We have to get out of here.'

My head was spinning as each step brought a bolt of pain up my leg. When we made it through the front door I felt the cold night air upon my face, and I am sure it was all that stopped me from fainting in fear, fright and pain.

The only way I was able to make it back to the buckboard was on the big broad back of Hollis. With my arms around his neck and hands clenched across his chest, he curled his forearms around my legs to act as stirrups, while I clung on tight and prayed to the Lord for forgiveness. Oh, what a fool I had been – shooting up cowhands and Texan gunslingers, playing mystery gunmen, and creeping around in the dark. The hard, cold reality of my foolhardiness had now caught up with me. Karl O'Brian, the man I once thought was my father and who had taken from me the Double U, had won. He may not have shot me, or caught me, but he knew it was me. He had heard Hollis call my name, I had called back, and he had my Henry rifle. What a pitiful state of affairs I had got myself into. I could now see that I was going to jail, or maybe I would be hanged as an example to other young women who would tread such a criminal path as mine. And what of Rita and Alex? Would they be drawn into this sordid affair? Oh dear, what could the matter be with me, to have allowed things to get to such a state as this?

18

BAD NEWS

Feeling No Pain

The next day was worse. Hollis said nothing, but I knew what he was thinking – why did he ever get mixed up with this stupid girl? We were going down, as they say in those popular detective drama magazines, which I would now have plenty of time to read when incarcerated for my crimes. It was now just a matter of waiting until the sheriff rode out to arrest us both.

When Sheriff Owen Reed did arrive, I was surprised that it had taken him three whole days. We saw him coming from afar. Hollis said nothing and nor did I. We just stood in the veggie patch, our eyes fixed and unblinking, as he rode slowly into view from over the horizon with dust drifting off behind him from his mount. I knew it was our comeuppance time. He cantered into the front yard and dismounted, slowly, taking his time to tie off his horse, and with no sense of haste he finally made his greeting.

I remember thinking how civil of him to lift his hat and hold it in both hands before he would say those fateful words. Nettie Youcheck you are under arrest. But he didn't say that at all, instead he said, 'Nettie, I have some bad news. Best you come up on the porch where you can sit down.'

I nearly blurted out I know why you are here, take me standing as I will have plenty of time to sit while in jail. However, I caught the look on Hollis's face from the corner of my eye and bit my lip. It was an expression that I knew so well, which seemed to say, 'Don't say anything you may regret.' Instead, I put my hoe down in the furrow and Hollis helped me limp to the front porch, where I sat upon the bench.

'I know of no other way to say this, so I'll just spit it out,' said our local sheriff.

I felt my regret well as tears of shame started to pool in my eyes.

'Your father is dead,' he said.

My immediate response was, *what!* And without thought, both hands sprang spontaneously from my lap and clutched at my cheeks as I burst into tears. Great big uncontrollable sobbing tears. The sort that flow from an adolescent in distress – only these were tears of both shock and sheer relief. Did I hear right? That bastard, Karl O'Brian, is dead. 'Are you sure?' I blubbered.

'I am, unfortunately, Nettie.'

'How could it be?' I heard my voice say but it didn't seem to come from me.

'Not sure of the exact circumstances. Seemed he fired a shot in the house that shattered a large mirror, then somehow slipped on the broken glass. In falling, he must have knocked himself out and cut both arms and a leg. And with no one to help, he just lay there and bled to death.'

'When did it happen?' asked Hollis respectfully.

'Not sure, really,' said the sheriff. 'His body was only found late yesterday and he had been dead awhile. We think maybe Saturday evening or even Sunday morning.'

'No one heard the shot from over in the bunkhouse?' asked Hollis carefully.

'The few hands that still work at the Double U were in town on the weekend. The only one around was Martha and she said she saw and heard nothing. In fact, she thought Karl was still in town also.'

I gathered my composure and wiped my nose on my sleeve. 'What now?' I asked.

'The body has been removed and is in town with the undertaker. You will need to speak to him regarding funeral arrangements.'

'Of course,' I said while trying not to smile with the sheer joy of it all.

Sheriff Reed waved his hat a little to indicate that he was about to go. 'Just one other difficult thing to discuss,' he said.

'Yes?' I said with a quiver of concern in my voice.

'The spot where your father died has left a terrible mess that needs to be cleaned up. The floor is going to need disinfecting. In fact, the whole homestead is a real mess with empty bottles everywhere and things lying around.'

'Hollis,' I said as sincerely as I could, 'we should go straight over and fix things, before we go to town to see the undertaker.'

A deferential agreement was murmured by Hollis in response.

The sheriff then advised, 'Even found one of the rifles just lying on the floor, a good-looking .44 Henry. I tried to put it back in the gun cabinet, but it was locked and I couldn't find the key.'

Quick as a flash, Hollis said, 'Is it the gun that Mister Karl fired the shot from?'

'No, the Henry hadn't been fired. It was as clean as a

143

whistle. The gun he used was with him. Karl must have got the Henry out but never put it back.' The sheriff paused before saying. 'I know one should never speak ill of the dead, but Nettie, your father had been drinking, heavily – and guns and whiskey don't mix.'

'Amen to that,' said Hollis, nodding his head in reverence.

We watched the sheriff ride away but in a different frame of mind as to how we had watched him arrive. The whole visit had taken no more than ten minutes. When he finally disappeared below the horizon, Hollis said, 'You can breathe out now.'

I turned to Hollis and we looked at each other as our lips slowly turned to smirks, then to smiles, and finally into uncontrollable laughter. Hollis started to do a jig and I got up and joined him, clumping our heels upon the veranda, while I grabbed and gripped his strong arms to stop from falling over, but I didn't feel any pain in my bad ankle, not even one tiny little twinge.

19

TRUST

Just Like My Mother

As we were getting on the buckboard to drive over to the Double U and then into town, I told Hollis to wait a minute. When I came back he saw that I was carrying Clement's Colt.

'What do you want that for?' he asked.

'Not sure, yet,' is all I said as I put it in the holding box under the seat.

He looked at me, concerned.

It was afternoon before we got into Grange. Hollis and I had first gone to examine the spot where Karl O'Brian had bled to death. The dried patch of blood was large and had congealed, drawing flies into the house and the smell reminded me of a dead rat, which seemed appropriate. We rolled up our sleeves, swept up the broken mirror where we could then washed and mopped the stain. 'Gonna take more than one go,' said Hollis.

'I know,' I said, but I didn't care how many goes it took. I was back in my home and this time no one was going to take it away from me.

We stopped outside Gilliam's Funeral Parlour. Mr Gilliam was expecting me as Sheriff Reed had informed him that he was riding out that morning to deliver the *sad* news.

Hollis had to dig me in the ribs at one stage when we were in the parlour and Mr Gilliam had left the room. 'Stop grinning,' he said in an earnest whisper.

'I didn't know I was grinning,' I said. 'At least, not that much.'

'Worse than that cat of Alice in the looking glass book.'

As soon as Hollis said looking glass and I thought of that shattered mirror, well, I started to get the uncontrollable giggles. Luckily, I had a linen handkerchief that I was able to stuff into my mouth until Mr Gilliam returned. He took one look at me biting on the linen and thought it was from the grief. 'There, there,' he said and gave me a pat on my shoulder. 'I know how upsetting this can be. You have seen much grief in your short life with the loss of a husband and a father.'

I daren't take the kerchief from between my teeth should I burst out giggling, while Hollis just rolled his eyes to the heavens.

From the funeral parlour we drove over to Rita's. As soon as she saw us, she bustled us both into her office without a word and closed the door. Her eyes were wide. 'What are you doing here?' Her words were fast and frantic.

'Karl is dead,' I said.

'I know, it's the talk of the town,' said Rita in a state.

'The sheriff rode over and told me and Hollis early this morning,' I said. 'It sure was a surprise.'

Rita looked confused. 'But you already knew.'

'Knew what?' I asked innocently.

'That he was dead.'

'No,' I said and looked over at Hollis. 'Took us by complete surprise.'

Rita put her hand to her mouth. 'But didn't you – I mean – I just assumed that you had shot him dead.'

I glanced across to check that the door was closed, and in a whisper I said, 'We were in the house when it happened, but we didn't do it. Didn't even know he had fallen over on the mirror glass. I thought the shot might have been for me.'

Rita's still looked perplexed. 'So, you didn't kill Karl O'Brian?'

Hollis and I shook our heads in unison.

'What great divine providence,' said Rita and plonked down into her chair. 'It is all over, at last. What a relief.'

'No, not yet,' I said. 'I still haven't got the Double U back.'

'But you will,' said Rita, 'who could stop you now?'

'I don't think anyone can, but I never thought anyone could take it away from me in the first place. This time I need to make sure it never happens again.'

'How?' said Rita.

'Yes, how precisely?' asked Hollis.

I looked up at the wall clock. 'I'm going over to the bank to have a word with Mr Albert Hopkins.'

'And say what?' said Rita.

'I've been thinking about that on the way into town.'

'I knew you were too quiet,' said Hollis. 'And when you go quiet and think, I worry.'

'I'm going to get the agreement made by my husband to stop Karl O'Brian laying claim to the Double U.'

'You can't do that, it could implicate young Alex, and besides,' scoffed Rita, 'what makes you think he will even acknowledge its existence, let alone give it to you?'

'Because if he doesn't, I will threaten to kill him.'

147

Hollis took in a long breath through his nostrils. 'Lordy,' he said, 'here we go again. That's why you fetched the Colt.'

'Have you thought this through, Nettie?' asked Rita.

'I think so.'

'Maybe we should go and see Lawyer Pruett and get a legal opinion first,' proposed Rita.

'That sounds like a good idea,' said Hollis, backing up Rita.

'Yes, I do need to see Pruett for advice, but it was legalities that lost me the Double U in the first place, so I no longer trust the law to provide justice. I need to pursue that myself, and on that account, you are going to have to trust that I know what I'm doing.'

Rita straightened her back and fixed her gaze upon me. 'I do, Nettie Youcheck, because you are just like your mother and I trusted her with my life.'

It was a lovely thing to say and I reached out and touched Rita's hand in a loving response.

Rita put her hand on mine and patted it. 'Would you like a nip of Irish before you confront Hopkins?' she asked.

'Should I?'

'One won't hurt. It'll help steady the nerves.'

Hollis rolled his eyes then shook his head.

'Just one, Hollis,' I said. 'To steady the nerves.'

20

CLEMENT'S COLT

A Matter of Trust

I went straight from Rita's to the office of Lawyer Pruett. He greeted me and offered his condolences as he shook my hand. Although I think he knew the death of Karl O'Brian was of no great loss from my life. The meeting was short and the advice I sought was provided with precise clarity. I asked him to repeat it, just in case there was a *however* – but there was not. He was unequivocal, my legal status was as both a widow and an orphan, therefore I was now the sole remaining legal beneficiary of the Double U. I bid goodbye with a sense of renewed confidence and made for the Grange Branch of the Missouri Savings and Loans Bank.

Alex Milton, who was standing next to the chief clerk, saw me enter the bank, and like Rita, he had just assumed that I was the one who had killed Karl O'Brian. His look was serious and seemed to express that danger was in the air. I said to Mr Mummery in a firm and clear voice that even surprised me, 'Could you advise the manager that I wish to discuss some urgent business with him, in person?'

In all honesty, I think it was the Irish talking.

Alex replied with confidence while looking at the chief clerk, 'I will deliver the message, Mr Mummery.'

Mummery looked a little taken back and timidly nodded his agreement.

Alex returned within the minute. 'He said he is presently busy.' Then added, 'Would you like to wait, Mrs Youcheck?'

I was not to be deterred. 'No, I won't. Take me to him, now.'

'We can't do that, Mrs Youcheck,' said Mummery submissively. 'You must understand, the manager is a busy man.'

'Too busy to see the widow of Clement Youcheck who was this bank's biggest customer; and too busy to see the grieving daughter of Karl O'Brian, who was also an important customer.'

'Well, I'm sure Mr Hopkins doesn't mean any disrespect, Mrs Youcheck.'

'Looks mighty ill-mannered to me,' I said, 'so best you take me to him now. I want no more than a few minutes of his time.'

Alex came to my aid. 'This way Mrs Youcheck, please follow me.'

Mummery looked relieved to have his junior seize the initiative.

I had placed Clement's Colt in the side pocket of my coat. It was a large pocket, but it still failed to fully hide the handgun as an inch or two of the handle stuck out at the top, which I had to conceal with the inside of my arm. It was also very heavy and pulled down on the right side of the coat from the shoulder. However, neither Mr Mummery nor Alex noticed.

When we arrived outside the manager's door, Alex went

to knock, but I didn't wait. I turned the doorknob and went straight in. Alex closed the door behind me.

The look on Albert Hopkins' face was priceless. It showed sheer surprise and a touch of fright, which gave me the assurance I needed. That, along with the Irish and Clement's Colt.

'Mrs Youcheck.' he said with astonishment.

'Mr Hopkins,' I replied with cool, calm clarity.

'How may I help?'

I sat down in front of his large desk, just as I had when I called to see him for a bank loan.

'Yes, please sit.' He sat down himself.

'Have you heard the news that my father is dead?'

'Yes, yes, and my sincere condolences.'

'First a widow, and now an orphan,' I said. 'And all before the age of twenty-one. So young.'

'I agree,' said Hopkins, not knowing what else to say.

'As the surviving wife and daughter of the previous legal owners, I will be taking over the management of the Double U, and in doing so, I will need your assistance.'

'The Missouri Savings and Loans Bank is always happy to help.'

'Not always,' I corrected.

Hopkins didn't respond and looked a little uncomfortable in his silence.

'But it's not the bank's assurance I want, it's yours, up front and personal, to me, Nettie Youcheck. Do you think you could do that?'

'My personal assistance? How?' he asked slowly.

I could sense that he was starting to relax a little and gain poise after my sudden and unannounced arrival. 'First,' I said, my voice still strong and maybe a little too loud. 'I'd like to show you something.' I pulled the Colt from my pocket and it made a heavy clunk as I plonked it on the edge of the big wide desk.

Hopkins' eyes bulged, and I knew I had not only gained his full attention but also regained the initiative.

'It was my husband's. He taught me how to shoot a handgun. I'm better with a rifle. In fact, some say I can shoot the whiskers off a flea from a fair way out. But I'm still pretty handy with a pistol. Reckon I could shoot any target in this room, big or small. Even on the run.'

Hopkins seemed frozen and couldn't stop staring at the pistol, lying on its side, the end of the barrel facing directly towards him.

'Why am I showing you this?' I paused to glance down at the revolver – a pause always works well for dramatic effect. 'Clement carried it for protection as the legal titleholder of the Double U, and I mean to do the same.' I paused again. 'And do you know why I know I'm the legal titleholder?' This time I didn't pause. 'Because Lawyer Pruett has told me so, this very day. The death of my father has removed any real or perceived impediments.'

The blood seemed to drain from Hopkins' face.

'But I need protection beyond that of a firearm,' I said. 'I need some trusted allies.'

Hopkins now looked a little confused.

'My husband taught me the importance of having a bank you can trust when running a business like the Double U. Especially, where capital is needed from time to time. And of course,' I leant forward a little, which seemed to spook Hopkins who pulled back in his chair, 'a bank needs good customers so that it may collect all those fees,' I smiled, before saying, 'Unfortunately, Clement never got to tell me of the importance of having a bank manager you can *trust*.' I emphasized that last word for effect. 'I guess my husband just took that for granted, believing a bank and a bank manager were one and the same.'

Hopkins' eyes remained fixed on the Colt, where he could look straight into the revolving chambers, each fully loaded.

'But somehow,' I continued, while trying to display all the confidence in my voice that I could muster, 'that *trust* got sort of lost along the way, so I'm here to get it back, along with an important document that you have down in your vault.'

I could see some small beads of sweat collecting on his brow. 'I have gone through the documents with you, Mrs Youcheck, there was nothing of any consequence held by the bank.' He was prevaricating in fine fibbing fashion, but his voice faulted a fraction.

'We are not off to a good start here,' I said, 'when it comes to the restoration of *trust*.' I placed my hand on the Colt with my trigger finger extended. 'Do you want to try again? I don't want to be here all day. I have a funeral to arrange.'

'I don't know what to else to say,' said Hopkins.

'I do,' I said.

He sat in silence.

'Why not just say that maybe the Double U deposit box could be checked again just in case something was missed the last time I was here.'

'I can assure you that we have never held a copy of your husband's will in this bank.'

'Let's just take one more look, shall we? Never know what we might find.'

Hopkins tried to smile, but it looked more like fright. 'Very well, I will look.' He tried to smile again. It still didn't work. 'Just for you, Mrs Youcheck.'

'Good,' I said, 'that's all I ask.'

Hopkins got up from his chair and gave the slightest of grins.

'And I will go with you,' I said as I stood up and took the

Colt in my hand. 'Please lead.'

The grin disappeared from Hopkins' face as he walked around the side of the desk, and after he had passed, I slipped the gun back into my coat pocket.

On arrival at the vault, the door was closed but unlocked. Hopkins pulled it open. As he entered, I called to Mummery, who was standing with his back turned, only a few feet away. 'Mr Mummery, would you please join us?'

'That won't be necessary, Mummery,' said Hopkins.

Mummery stopped and went to turn away.

'I asked Mr Mummery to join us, please attend to my wishes,' I said as I slid my hand into my pocket and felt the smooth cold surface of the big iron.

A drop of sweat began to trickle down the side of Hopkins' face near the temple. He was trapped, and he knew it.

'In fact, Mr Mummery, would you open the safe deposit box that rightfully belongs to my deceased husband, please?'

Mummery responded as a diligent employee. 'Of course, Mrs Youcheck,' he said, 'I'd be pleased to be of assistance.' He crossed to the register, took it from the shelf, opened the book, located the name Youcheck, identified the number, drew the key and went to the box. He extracted it from the wall and laid it upon the table in the centre of the vault.

I waited.

'Open it,' said Hopkins reluctantly.

Mummery inserted the key and lifted the lid.

'Please take out everything and lay it on the table,' I said, and my mouth was getting a little dry but not for water. I had the strong desire for another shot of Irish, just to settle the nerves.

The contents were laid out one at a time, slowly, which

gave me the opportunity to casually point to each and say, 'What's that?'

Mummery quickly answered, 'Old loan documents and title deeds.'

'And those?'

'Bonds, railroad bonds.'

'Valuable?' I asked.

'Very much so,' said Mummery as he lifted out a stack of brand new bank bills bound by a paper band with the sum of $5,000 written upon it in Indian ink.

'Now that could have come in handy,' I said.

Finally, the last piece of paper, folded in half, was drawn from the bottom of the box.

I pointed to it. 'And that?'

'I'll deal with that one,' said Albert Hopkins. 'You may go, Mr Mummery.'

Mummery got the message and seemed relieved that he could go.

I waited until he was out of earshot. 'Would you like to read that to me, aloud?'

Albert Hopkins seemed most reluctant to take up the single folded page, instead dropped his head to stare at the floor. 'No need, Mrs Youcheck,' he said. 'It states that your father never had any legal claim over the Double U. He forfeited that right to your husband.' Hopkins gave a small exasperated moan as he looked up to see the smile on my face. 'You don't seem surprised?'

I was ready for this question, but needed to be careful that I was not too clever with my prepared fib. 'I'm not,' I said.

'Can I ask who told you of its existence?'

'My husband,' I lied, 'but not while he was alive. I found reference to it in Clement's cash ledger along with a note in his diary on the day the payment was made. It said that an agreement had been made prior to his forthcoming marriage, and that it would be held in the bank for safe keeping if ever needed.'

'And when did you find this out?'

'Only this very morning when tidying up the mess left from my father's—' I paused a little before adding, '*accident*. I was returning documents and journals back to my husband's desk when I chanced upon the entry. Why he had never mentioned this agreement to me I can only guess. Maybe, he thought it was for the better, to hide from me his lack of trust in my father.' I glanced around the vault before saying, 'I wish he had, as I never trusted my father either.'

Hopkins gave a solemn nod his head.

'I will now take this document and secure it myself.'

Hopkins eyes instantly showed panic as I reached and took up the sheet of paper from the desk. 'What are you going to do with it?' he asked. 'Show it to Lawyer Pruett? If you do, it will be—'

I cut him short. 'There is no need to show it to Lawyer Pruett as it has no bearing on the future. In a legal sense this document is no longer relevant as the agreement is between two parties which are now deceased.' I gave the piece of paper a little wave. 'It is redundant as I am now the legal owner of the Double U, regardless of my age.'

Hopkins' face showed a visible mix of confusion and relief.

I didn't trust Hopkins any more than I trusted the man who I thought was my father for all those years, but I wanted him to know that he was now held to ransom. Knowledge of the agreement would destroy him, should it ever be made known to the law. He had given evidence, under oath, to the contrary. But was this blackmail of mine risky? Not really. The Double U was a prime source of

income to the bank, and as manager he was paid hand-
somely to serve that account well. However, I could still see
that Hopkins was a little confused and having trouble
keeping up with all that had just gone down, so I said, 'I
trust that all will be fine from here on in. Don't you?'

'Yes, yes,' said Hopkins quickly.

'Well, why don't we start by ensuring that my railroad
bonds and equities remain safe and secure as I wish to use
them as surety for a loan. The Double U will need an injec-
tion of capital to bring it back into shape. As for the cash,
that will be required for the purchase of breeding stock to
rebuild our herd.'

'Yes, yes, of course,' said Hopkins, who actually gave a
little bow.

I could see the look of relief on the bank manager's
face, and I supposed that it was on mine, too, but he didn't
seem to notice. Hopefully, I had pulled off this charade
and put him in my debt; and that is where all bank man-
agers should be, in debt to their customers.

As I turned to leave, with the agreement in my hand, I
caught sight of Alex Milton by the vault door. This young
man had been so instrumental in this conclusion. I lifted
the folded paper in my hand, just a fraction, and winked at
him. He dropped his head slightly and coughed with his
fist to his mouth, before saying, 'And a very good day to
you, Mrs Youcheck.'

To which I replied, 'Thank you. It has been a very good
day already.'

21

A WILD CHILD

Nevada, Missouri – 1950

So, there it is. I have set the record straight and told the story as it was. Well, at least as best as I can recall after all these years, but I should know, I was there, wasn't I? Nowadays, of course, I am the only one left to reveal those happenings, so you will have to take me at my word.

The others have all gone.

The wonderful Hollis, who remained faithful to me and I to him, is long gone. So too is Rita, as is Lawyer Pruett, along with Albert Hopkins, who was to behave himself right up to the time he left Grange and went to Springfield to care for his ailing mother. Dutch Bonner, he's long gone too, and even the wonderful Alex Milton. He passed of tuberculosis nearly twenty years ago in Joplin. Or was it Ballwin? I forget now. But I miss him and his courage. I will always remain in his debt. In fact, I remain in all their debts.

I am the last one left now, just me, so it is important that things be told, especially the right things, to put to rest the gossipmongers and the likes of that wretched reporter

158

from St Louis who wrote that hurtful article in the *Enquirer*. He wasn't there, so how would he know. He just printed second hand tittle-tattle. I did not bankrupt the Double U, it was the great depression, and in particular the winter of 1932–33. No one in the valley came out unscathed. But, that's all in the past. I am at a time in my life where I just need to rest and reflect on the glory that was, and I don't mind saying that I have lived an exciting life.

I have been asked if I would still like to be at the Double U and I say, no. I like being here at Number 3. Living in these beautiful surrounds of Vernon County is so peaceful and beautiful to the eye, and not to mention how prestigious it is. Ours is the most handsome of places, although talk of removing the towers and trim from the main building is just plain foolish. This is my home and it is a grand home, so I will not allow it. The towers must stay, I say. Then there are the visits to the tearooms in Nevada. It is such a nice town. The nicest in the county, and bigger than Grange.

'Nettie?' came the call. Then a little more forcefully, 'Nettie?'

'Oh, you startled me.'

'I didn't meant to, Nettie. I thought you were asleep.'

'No, not asleep, just resting.'

'Time for your medication.'

'Is that you, Clement, my love?'

'No,' came the soft response.

'Of course not, I just got a little confused for a moment. Clement has gone, and so has Hollis.'

Two strong young hands clasped then rubbed my frail fingers. 'If you could see properly, then you'd know it's me, David.'

'David?'

The young man in the white uniform leant in close so

that I could hear him. 'Yes, David.'

'Of course it is, David.'

'As soon as you take your medication I can read to you if you like. Maybe, something back from the days when you were young. You like those stories, don't you?'

'When I was young?' I said whimsically.

'Yes, when you were young.'

'I was young once, and I had such an exciting life.'

'I know, you've told me. You were a wild child. You've told me lots of stories.'

'I have, haven't I.'

'Yes, back in the old days.'

'I could tell you a thing or two about the days of the Old West.'

'You have, but tell me again while I clean up your room.'

'I was young and pretty then, but still, people dismissed me out of hand because I was a girl with no mother and a drunkard who was not my real father. Anyway, I showed them. I showed them all. I was a dark horse. That was back when I was taking potshots at the cowhands. Would you like to hear that one? How I saved the Double U?'

'Yes,' said the orderly in his neat whites at the Number 3 Missouri State Hospital. 'I like that story very much.'